# THE BALLAD OF BILLY BADASS

A Novel By

## PATRICK SHEANE DUNCAN

Encyclopocalypse Publications
www.encyclopocalypse.com

# THE BALLAD OF BILLY BADASS

# CHAPTER ONE

Hot night. Muggy.

Hot wet, wool blanket laying over the land. Michigan in July. 1951. Blueberry bushes. Row upon row. Five, six feet high. Trimmed for a picker's reach. Separated by plowed earth. Dirt powder and clods.

A full moon. Casts all into blue, gray and black.

Two men charge through the bushes. Arms in front of faces. Charge at a diagonal. Busting brush. Flail for balance. Charge the next. Attacking the columns of bush. One after another. Kick dust into a low-level fog.

Suddenly burst into the open. Stop under black tree shade. Access road. Forest beyond. Chests heave, gulp air, lungs burn. Guts cramped. Sweaty faces plastered with leaves and dirt, arms. Scratches bleed, blood fading in sweat.

One man, big, wide, severe crew cut. Flattop level as a rule. The other thin, face all bones. Pointy chin, blade nose, cheekbones sharp. Black hair Brilliantined shiny as a ten-inch record. "Brylcreem, a little dab'll do ya."

Silence for a moment. The men listen. Crickets cheep, frogs squeak. Solos, then chorus. "Creek, creek, creek."

Something else. Voices. Laughter. Muted. Rhythmic. A radio.

The two men step into the forest. Maples and dogwood. Dogwood flowers impersonate the crucifixion. Once a year. Blood on white petals.

The hardwood segues to pine. Carpet of needles below. Every footstep cushioned. Quiet. Brylcreem snaps a branch underfoot. Crack! Crewcut cast pale blue eyes on him. Brylcreem grins. Yellow varnished teeth. Tobacco-stained circle inscribed on front teeth.

Crewcut points. A glow ahead. The radio louder. A backyard. House ahead. White siding florescent under moonlight. Yellow light from windows. Light and laughter spill out open back door, filtered by a screen door.

The men move forward. Wary of a dog. One bark and they will run. No dog. Walk past a child's swing set. Red and yellow paint bright and new.

Crew cut stops short of puddle of light. Stays in the shadow. Holds Brylcreem back with big meaty hand. Peers through screen door. Can see open front door through house. Another screen. Cross ventilation on a hot night. Not much help tonight. No wind. Kitchen dark. Light coming from a side room. Bedroom? Source of the radio.

Both men wait. Both wear khakis, pants and shirts. Sweat stained. Dirty. Torn. No belts. Large "P" stenciled on the shirt back. They listen for a moment. Mario Lanza show, sponsored by Coca-Cola. Crewcut dreamed of cold Cokes in prison. Like in the ads. Dewed bottles, cold enough to make your teeth ache.

One story house. Tiny. Shotgun shack. No garage. '50 Nash station wagon in gravel driveway. Two wheeled, red kids scooter dumped against back porch. Crew cut smiles. Twitches end of his mouth, then gone.

Brylcreem tests screen door. Locked. Crewcut laughs to himself. A locked screen door. Tits on a boar. Elbows Brylcreem aside. Reaches into back pocket. Stabs screen with sharpened screwdriver. Weeks of grinding tip on concrete floor. Blood on plastic handle. Brylcreem a look out.

Crewcut slices through the metal net. Screen rips. Loud. Too loud? He stops. Listens. Breath held. Crickets and frogs. Mario's special guest Kay Starr on the radio. Breathe again. Slides hand into the cut. Feels for latch. A blind snake poking for food.

Clack. Door opens. Slight hinge squeak. Step into the kitchen. Clean. Four chairs and Formica table. Matching. Dishes still wet on the rack. Smells of fried food. Hot milk. Stirs Crewcut's stomach juices. Brylcreem follows.

Crewcut pries open fridge. Slow. Spills light on to checkerboard linoleum floor. Grabs quart jug of milk. Gulps from the wide mouth. Presses cold bottle against face. Forehead. Cheeks. Blessed Jesus. Drinks more. Cool liquid spills down chin, neck. Not a Coke but sweet relief.

Brylcreem eases open drawers. Stealth sorts through utensils.

Shadow fills the doorway. Everybody frozen.

"Oh, sweet Lord." A woman. Man's shirt. Open. No panties. A real blonde.

Crewcut gets hard. Instant erection. Stainless steel. She's a plain bitch. Not homely. Not ugly. Terrified. Carries a cat. Orange tabby. Yellow eyes. Drops it. Cat scurries away. Claws skitter on linoleum.

"Well, fuck me gently..." Brylcreem stares at snatch. Mesmerized.

Crewcut acts fast. Grabs the bitch by the neck. One hand. Sits her in a chair. Puts a grimy finger to his wet lips. Milk dribble on his chin. Same hand holds the screwdriver. Her eyes fix on the scratched steel.

She quivers with fear. Cold shivers. Sees Brylcreem. Frozen at the drawers. Her eyes flit from man to man. Back and forth. Like a bird tests its cage. Bounce about the wire.

Fridge still hangs open. Light casts big shadows on the walls.

Kay Starr moans, "While the wheel keeps spinning, spinning, spinning…"

"Damn, babe, can't you even manage to put the damn cat…" The husband steps into the kitchen. Boxer shorts and slippers. White chest, few dark hairs. Tanned face and cuffs. Carries the damned cat. Freezes.

Crewcut flicks on the light switch. Motions husband to a chair. He looks at wife. She looks to him. Eyes begging.

The husband steps to the table. Doesn't sit. Thinking. Dangerous that. Still holds the damned cat.

"While the wheel is turning, turning, turning…"

Crewcut taps husband with the shank.

"Be quiet. Be nice. We need things. Clothes. Food. Some cash. The keys to your car."

Brylcreem oblivious to the men. Sidles over to the woman. Slides woman's shirt aside. Exposes a breast. Large dark nipple. Silver dollar areola. Brylcreem rubs a knuckle across. Skin puckers. Nipple contracts.

Brylcreem leers. "Maybe some pussy. Know how long it's been since I even seen some nookie?"

HOWL-SCREECH-YOWL. Husband hurls cat at Crewcut. Crewcut catches with his face. Crewcut howls. Much like the cat.

Husband spins. Snatches knife from open drawer. Thrusts blade into Brylcreem's chest. At same second. Crewcut tears ball of teeth and claws from his face. Pitches beast through kitchen window.

Glass shatters.

Then quiet. Stillness. No one knows what to do next. Husband has no plan past this. Crewcut takes in scene. Looks to Brylcreem. At knife stuck in chest.

Brylcreem stares at same thing. Winces.

Husband and wife stare at Brylcreem. Transfixed.

Brylcreem goes through some changes. Dumb befuddlement. Some pain. Then the old fall back. Anger.

Brylcreem yanks blade from chest. Sucking sound. Brylcreem roars. Slashes across husband's throat. Husband reacts. Too slow. Steps back too late. Dark red line across neck seeps blood. Then gushes. Pulses with heartbeat. Hands go to throat. Blood leaks between fingers. He falls on his ass. Sits there. Looks annoyed. Teeters over sideways. Eyes going blank.

Brylcreem looks from husband to Crewcut.

"Ain't that a bitch?" Looks down at his chest. Gingerly touches cut. Pulsing with bloody froth.

"It's not that deep." Brylcreem muses.

And he lists a bit. One knee folds. Goes to both knees. Puzzled expression. The big question.

Crew cut steps toward Brylcreem. His only friend. Not really friend. Cell mate. Companion. Collaborator. Friend, maybe.

Brylcreem starts to fall. Forward. Crewcut doesn't want him to hit face down. Takes step to catch the man. His friend.

The wife bolts. Breaks for the living room.

Crewcut dashes after. Grabs at her. Fist full of shirt. Rips. Tears. She falls. Scrambles. Desperate. Crawls across carpet. On all fours.

Crewcut tackles her. Climbs over her. Groin against butt. Naked pumping butt. Legs working. Crewcut's hard-on back. Returns like a motherfucker. Rolls her on her butt.

Holds her down. Tiny arms in his big fists. She struggles. Writes against him. Tits roil. He eyes them. First real tit in twelve years. She makes sounds. With clenched teeth, lips together. Kitten mews.

He releases one arm. Rips open pants. Frees cock. Her free hand claws at his face. Pummels him. He recaptures. She tries to knee him. He dodges. They writhe. Battle. Coffee table goes over. Cascade of magazines. Wrapped hard candies.

Cock slips inside. Wet. Warm. Hot even. She stops fighting. Sags. Limp. Surrenders. He stops. Doesn't move. Afraid to move. Will come instantly. Let's loose one of her hands. Slowly. Her arm lies there. He wipes mouth with back of hand. Spit on his chin.

He looks down at her. Blue eyes. Unfocused. Looking into space. Past the ceiling. Above the roof. Beyond this place. This moment.

Crewcut places one hand over a breast. Soft. And firm. Squeezes. Fondles nipple. No response. Runs hand down to belly. Stretch marks. But firm. Blonde cunt hair. Thick.

He thrusts. She might as well be dead. Thrusts again. Her body buffeted. But still nothing.

He wants something. See me! Feel this! Goddammit, I'm here!

He kisses her. Tongue explores. Acknowledge me!

She wakes. Eyes widen. Eyes roll. All white. Staring at her own brain.

Screams. Wail erupts from her mouth. Wide and loud. Twists her neck. Head jerks back and forth.

Won't stop screaming. Hand over her mouth. Scream muffled. Other hand on neck. Curls around her throat. She struggles. Moves under him.

Better. Much better. He plunges. Cock deep. Pelvis to pelvis. Again. Again. Harder. Harder. Beyond stopping. Pleasure like a hot wave. Engulfed.

He arches neck. Breathes through clenched teeth.

Eyes closed. Concentrating. Dwelling in the pure, perfect pleasure. The sweet feeling swells. A crimson bubble grows from groin to brain. Bursts. Relief. His whole body spasms.

He opens his eyes. Sees the woman's face. Purple. Eyes bloodshot. Staring at nothing. Dead. Body limp.

Crewcut pulls away. Hand from her mouth. Hand from her throat. Impressions of his fingers on her skin. Her head flops. Dead eyes stare at the floor. Mouth slack.

Crewcut on his knees. Tucks in. Dick wet. Sticky. Buttons pants.

"Mama?"

Crewcut turns. A child. Four, five maybe. Pajama bottoms. In the bedroom doorway. Looking at the dead woman.

"Mama?"

# CHAPTER TWO

Driving. South. Headlights carve out a path in the dark. Steering with one hand. The other buttons a shirt. Too small. Gives up. Turns on the radio. Dash lights glow. Radio warms up. Hank Williams. Hank always fits.

"No matter how I struggle and strive, I'll never get out of this world alive."

Looks across the seat. The kid. Huddled against the door. Eyes the man. Hand on the door handle.

"Get away from the fucking door."

Kid doesn't move.

"Dangerous."

Kid just watches. White-blond hair over eyes. Needs a haircut. Crewcut leans over. Grabs fistful of hair. Drags kid across the seat. Kid fights. Pounds with tiny fists.

Crewcut releases. Drapes arm over kid's neck. Holds the boy in place. Pressed against side. Kid sinks teeth into his arm. Hurts.

The man backhands the brat.

Kid doesn't cry. Just sits. Stares at Crewcut. Man looks at bite marks. Grins.

"Regular Billy Badass. Ain'tcha"

* * *

1956. From glaring sunlight to dim tavern. Barflies shrink from the glare. Vampires. Just another bar. Smell of stale beer, acid wine. Jukebox crooning. Gogi Grant.

Louisville.

Dusty photos of Kentucky Derby on walls. The boy likes horses. Pass them on the road. In buses. Stolen cars.

Crewcut and boy at bar. Crewcut sports sideburns. Boy with identical hair. Surgical crewcut and sideburns. Crewcut in brown leather bomber jacket. Stolen in Chicago. Passed out wino. Wino woke up. Crewcut beat him back to unconsciousness.

Kid's clothes too small. All wrists and ankles. Grows too fast.

Crewcut lifts boy onto bar. Kid stands tall. Fists on hips. Scans bar with bad intent. Little Rascals tough.

"Who's the meanest motherfucker in this joint?!" Little voice gone loud. Big balls. Bulldog jaw juts.

Barfly nudges buddy. Snarks. Plays along. "I am!"

Kid fixes him with pugnacious sneer.

"Then you best scram. 'Cause I'm taking over." Barflies chuckle. Crewcut loves it. Prods the boy. "Who are you?"

"I'm Billy Badass!"

"How mean are you?"

"There's three things you don't do; Piss against the wind, French kiss a rattle snake, and fuck with me!"

More laughter.

Crewcut lowers Billy to a stool.

Bartender steps to face them. Crewcut takes his cue. "Pabst. And a Coke. Put a cherry in it."

"Kid's a tough little snot."

"Ain't he though."

Bartender pours the beer. Adds some cherry juice to the Coke. Crewcut elbows Billy.

"How tough are you?"

"Tougher than woodpecker lips. Eat the boogers outa a dead man's nose." Billy fishes in the Coke with dirty fingers. Forages for the cherry.

Bartender winks at a patron. Pours a shot of whiskey. Sets it next to the Coke.

"All the tough guys in here drink Four Roses."

Crewcut rolls himself a Bull Durham. Just watches. Billy looks to him.

"Thank the man."

"Thanks mister."

Billy picks up the shot glass. Raises it to his lips. Wrinkles his nose at the smell. Smells like Crewcut does. Boy takes a tiny sip. Twists up face. Puts the glass down. Tries to spit. Awful.

"Drink it like a man." Crewcut says it soft. Dangerous when he's quiet.

"Tastes like shit." Kid juts out jaw again.

"Don't embarrass me in front of all these folks."

"Fuck you." That usually gets a laugh. Not tonight.

"Put up your dukes."

Fear in the boy's eyes. Raises fists. Up in front of face. Little knuckles white. Crewcut squats. Face-to-face.

Everybody in the bar watches.

"You get first punch."

Billy taps Crewcut on the jaw.

"C'mon. Like a man. Not a fucking pussy."

Billy swings. Lands a good one. Right below the man's eye. Crewcut blinks. Startled. Grins. The kid is learning. Fuck the mouth. Teeth hurt your hands. Go for the eyes.

Smacks the boy right off the stool. Upside the kid's head. Boy sprawled on floor. Amid spit and peanut shells.

"Hey, mister." Bartender leans over. Checks out the kid. "Folks round here we don't cotton to…"

Crewcut whirls. Stares the man quiet.

Billy's eyes fill with water. Nose trickles blood. Crewcut kneels down. Shoves face at boy.

"C'mon. Get up ya little pussy. Ya never quit a fight."

Billy rises. Painfully. Trying to trump the fear.

Suddenly charges Crewcut. Fists flail. Some connect. Crewcut takes the blows. In the face.

"Okay. Okay. I give. Uncle goddammit."

Billy stops. Snorting blood and snot. Sleeve wipe. Crewcut lifts boy back onto stool.

The kid eyes the shot glass.

"You ain't gotta drink it. You won."

Crewcut downs the shot. Chases it with beer. Eyes the bartender.

"Ain't he somethin'? Kid don't take shit. No how. No way. From nobody."

* * *

Shabby room. Shabby hotel. Billy contemplates the wallpaper. Imagining monsters in the water stains. A bear, reared up, roaring. A porcupine. Saw one in the mountains, sleeping on a picnic bench. A stagecoach. A cat after a butterfly. Saw that too. Cat ripped the wings, ate the bug.

Window open. Faded curtain dances. A woman snores. Sprawled on bed. Hard face. Cheeks pitted. Yellow hair. Black roots. Eyebrows two black pencil slashes. Lipstick smear on chin. Mouth open. Breasts slack puddles of white flesh. Purple concave nipples. Bite mark on tit. Dirty gray sheet across swollen gut.

Toilet flushes. Crewcut yanking up boxer shorts. Buttons shirt. Slides on pants. Shoes. Buckles belt. Jacket next. .45 automatic from side table. Into jacket pocket.

Kid watches with squinted eyes. Slept in two chairs pushed together. Seat to seat. Curled around blanket. Fully dressed.

Crewcut backhands boy's butt.

"Wake up and piss, the world's on fire."

Billy untangles from blanket. Rises. Rubs eyes. Shoves chairs apart. Puts on shoes. Looks at the woman.

"Learn anything last night?"

Kid rolls back memory. Crewcut and woman rutting. Boy watched. Woman protested. Crewcut slapped her quiet.

Billy coughs up loogie. Spits it onto magazine on the floor. *True Detective*. Woman was reading it. Her place. Other magazines. *True Romance, Secret*.

Crewcut whacks him. Back of the head. Teeth click. Bites tongue.

"Told ya, No spittin' indoors."

Billy pisses. Crewcut rifles woman's purse. Pockets her keys. Couple of wrinkled bills.

"C'mon."

Billy follows to door. Grabs handful of Cheetos. Chugs last of RC Cola.

"Don't drink that. It's flat."

"I like it flat." Billy defiant. Always. Crewcut smiles. Proud.

* * *

Her car is a '49 Hudson. Still nice inside. Crewcut lays pistol on seat. Between him and boy. Taught boy to shoot. Cans. Bottles. Old television tube found in an alley. Imploded. Big fun. Shot a squirrel once. Safety. Aim. Eyes open. Later disassemble. Clean. Put back together. Bigger fun for boy. Army style. Army vet Crewcut. Double-you double-you two. Slide bullets into clip. Shoot. Reload. Shoot. Clean. Reload. Shoot until boy didn't flinch. Big gun. Barely hold it up at first. Shoot until his ears rang for days. Fun.

Gun stolen from bar in North Carolina. Broke in. Sun coming up. Nobody on streets. Just the two of them. In the whole wide world. Cash hidden in cigarette machine. Crewcut knew all the tricks. Took cigarettes, too. Sold some in Pennsylvania.

Most of the time didn't need tricks. Just gun and run.

Back roads Ohio. Mom and Pop store. Gas pumps out front. Middle of nowhere. Crewcut's favorite. Kid stays in the car.

At first Crewcut put him in trunk. Boy hated that. Pounded, kicked. Screamed. Until he heard shots. Then whined and bitched. Promised to stay put. Next time.

Plenty of next times. Kid knew routine. Watched through the windows. Went in a couple of times. Stores all the same. Crowded with goods. Little of everything.

Crewcut walks to counter. Asks for Blue Blades. Man fetches Gillette Blue Blades. Crewcut drops fiver. Man punches the cash register key. Cash drawer opens.

Crewcut pulls his gun. Big gun. Man backs up. Crewcut pillages cash drawer. Stuffs pocket with fist full of money. Even takes the coins. Spots bank bag under counter. Grabs it.

"No. Please. That's my deposit." The man pleads.

Crewcut hates the begging. Gun clubs the man. Beats him to the floor.

Grabs a Dr Pepper on the way out. And a beer. And a can of Spam. Spam and Ritz crackers. For lunch. Back in the car. Pops bottle cap on the door. Billy drinks. Happy.

Crewcut drives. Cruise through tiny town. Past a school. Kids at recess. Playing. Laughing. A girl screams. In delight. A pleasant sound.

Billy looks away. Soda tastes like acid. Pours it out the window. Hurls bottle at road sign. Smashes. Likes that sound.

Crewcut hands him pistol.

"Clean it."

Boy wipes blood from the pistol. Finds skin chunk on sight. Hairs attached.

Not the first time.

Better than stuffed into trunk.

# CHAPTER THREE

1958. Minnesota. Fall. Late fall. Leaves about gone. Trees naked. Wind bitter.

Farm fields empty. Yellow corn stubs. Sky gray. Flat land. Desolate road. Sun sneaking down.

Riding in a semi. Crewcut shotgun. Billy in the bed behind the seats. Cab too hot.

Johnny Cash on the radio. Billy sings along. Trying to drown out shouting. Driver versus Crewcut. Crewcut drunk. Drunk a lot lately.

Stupid argument. Peterbilt versus Kenworth. Mack truck is for pussies.

Crewcut reaches for gun. Kid stiffens. But no gun. Hocked for pint of Kentucky Gentleman.

Semi comes to sudden stop. Hissing, grinding, screeching. Passenger door yanked open. Gust of cold air. Crewcut tumbles out. Billy climbs down on his own.

"Fuck you!" Crewcut screams at Driver. "Fuck you and the big white horse you rode in on!"

"Like I said, I ride a fucking Peterbilt!" The Driver yells. Slams door shut. Semi roars away. More hissing. Grinding through the gears. Red taillights shrink and disappear.

"Cocksucker." Crewcut curses the taillights. "Fucking cunt."

Crewcut and Driver argued about the boy. Should be in school. Crewcut's motto: School is for pussies. Besides he's drunk. Any excuse for an argument. Hoping for a fight. Likes to fight. Doesn't have to win. Doesn't a lot lately. Always with a cut over the eye. A swollen lip. Battered knuckles. Used to fight like a demon. Scared his opponent. Rage and ruthlessness. Dirty and mean. Not so possessed the last year. "Tired," he says. Tired all the time.

"Probably a fucking fairy," he says to the empty road. Hugs himself against the chill. Plunging temperature. Soon as sun goes down. Fucking cold just like that.

"We don't need shit like that." Crewcut mumbles.

"Fucking A," Billy says. To please the man.

Crewcut zips up. Wearing only a windbreaker. Boy's matches. Billy shivers. Breath fogs. They were heading south. Fleeing winter. Wind picks up. Naked branches rattle. Skeleton applause.

Crewcut props up his collar. Billy imitates. Out of habit.

"Asshole." Crewcut can't let it go. Weaves down center of tarmac. Billy follows. Huddled inside windbreaker. Bad name for coat. Wind cuts right through the motherfucker. Stabbing skin. Jams hands into pant pockets. Deep. Finds furnace of his groin. The fire is down.

Crewcut stops. Looks around. Nothing moves but lonely leaves. Sticks out thumb. Road is deserted. Looks at own thumb.

"Nothing comin'. Let's sack out."

Heads off road. To the ditch. Kicks up leaves. Checks. Dry. Sits/falls down. Pats the patch next to him.

"C'mere. We'll play spoons."

They've done this before. Slept outside. Haystacks. Beaches. Parks. A cemetery.

Billy crawls into Crewcut's lap. Man wraps his arms around boy's chest. Hugs kid.

"Gotten big." Boy has been growing. Ankles and wrists stick out from clothes.

"Need to go shopping." Crewcut shivers. Boy sleeps.

* * *

The boy awakes. Blind. Everything white. Saw blind man once. Milky eyes. This is what the blind man sees. Panics. Raises hand to eyes. Encounters snow. Wipes it away. Rises. White everywhere. White landscape. Brilliant white. Glaring white. Snowed overnight. Bright sun bounces off sheets of snow.

He is cold. So cold. Shivering. Snot running. Ears hurt. Fingers and toes ache.

Looks to Crewcut. No breath. Boy's breath is visible mist. Man's face flat white. Blue tinges. Boy has to pry Crewcut's arms apart. Frees self. Stares at the dead man. Blows breath out again. Sees mist. Checks man again. No fog. No breath.

Stares at dead man. Long time. Long time. So cold.

Reaches out hand. Toward bristly face. Stops short. Pulls hand back. Sticks it into armpit.

Climbs out of ditch. Stands on shoulder of road. One last look at curled up body. Mouth open. Arms curled out. Hugging air. Reaching? Begging? Crewcut never begged.

Boy turns. Walks away. Stomps feet. Flaps hands. Trying to get blood to flow. Walks fast to warm up. Keeps walking.

Heads down black top. Walks for miles. Snow melts on the road. Shoes wet. Feet cold. Walks for miles. No cars. A tractor once. Hauling empty trailer. Didn't stop.

Walks alone. Alone. For first time. Feels empty. Hears a car. Far away. Gradually louder. Leaky muffler. Billy spots it. On horizon. Coming at him.

Switches to other side of the road. Sticks out thumb. Car gets closer. Beat up Chevy station wagon. Texas plates. Riding low on springs. Roof piled with boxes, suitcases. Roped down.

Passes boy. Glimpse of faces. Kids stare at Billy. Chevy stops behind him.

Billy runs up. Six kids. Four adults. All Mexican. No room.

Engine rattles and rumbles. Kids prattle in English/Spanish. Adult woman chides driver in Spanish. Billy doesn't understand. Arguing for or against him? Never finds out.

Front door opens. Woman in front slides over. Makes room for Billy. Gestures to him. He climbs in. Closes door. Car drives off.

Warm in car. Woman looks him up and down.

"How far you go?" woman asks him.

Billy shrugs. Woman lets it go.

Drive past Crewcut's body. Nobody else notices. Billy cranes neck. Did the man protect him from the cold? Did he care? Billy ponders this. For years. Until the day he dies.

* * *

Peppered with questions. From the back seat and front. From kids and adults.

Parents?

Dead. Who he means by this he isn't sure.

Other family?

None.

Discussion ensues. Mostly in Spanish. Drop him off to police?

Question for Billy or someone else? Billy answers anyway. Don't want nothing to do with police.

Runaway?

Not running from anything.

Just drop him off somewheres.

Okay.

What will you do?

Keep hitchin'.

To where?

Dunno.

You stay with us 'til we figure this out. Okay.

You'll have to earn your keep. Work.

I can work.

Okay, then.

Simple as that.

* * *

The family takes him in. Rambling old farmhouse in Texas. Outside San Antonio. Pantry cleaned out. Given mattress and blankets. Sent to school with Saenz kids. Works before school. Weekends. Topping onions. Yank onions out of ground by tops. Cut off greens with sheep shears. Crawl along rows. Drag crate behind. Ten cents a crate. Papa Saenz keeps money. School days at field before sunup. Top onions for two hours. Clean up for school. Have to keep shears sharp. Always cutting hands. Onion juice in cuts. Stings like a motherfucker. Not supposed to say that anymore. Back aches. Bent over all the time. Ground wet from dew. Muddy. Dirty work. Never complains.

After onions, then Christmas trees. Trimming. Before school again. Walk around tree, swinging machete. Cutting into perfect tree shape. Later cutting and hauling. Machete work dangerous. Slip on wet fungus, dewy pine needles. Cut self. Swing too hard. Cut through battered shin guards. One kid almost cuts off own leg. Right through shin bone. Good football player. Career over. Haul trees to trucks. Run through bagger. Tossed on truck. Merry Christmas to somebody.

His Christmas. One present under tree. Other kids have multiples. He is grateful for the one. Clothes from Salvation Army. He is okay with that.

Works in green houses in winter. Hot work. He likes the heat. Hates the cold. Always will. Dream of that ditch. Wakes up shivering.

Enters school. No report cards. No birth certificate. Mama

Saenz pleads with Principal. School relents. Deals with immigrants every year. Illegals with no papers. Mama Saenz says parents dead. Car accident. Needs last name.

Mama Saenz asks. Last name?

Billy.

Billy what?

Billy Badass.

No. Billy what?

Billy Badass.

Tell Principal. Billy Bad.

Billy becomes William.

Bad becomes Budd. Mama's accent. Principal's joke? Bad hearing?

William Budd. Billy Budd. Doesn't realize until years later.

Likes school. Learns to read. Teachers treat like he is retarded. Mute child. Speaks rarely. Loves to read. When school is out, not working, lives in library. Loves the library. Always warm there.

Reads his way through volumes. All of the Hardy Boys. Tom Swift. The entire Science Fiction section. Then all the mysteries. Westerns. Loves books. Takes him away. Places. Biography. Reading other people's lives. Reads about families. Families. But viewing from outside. Always outside.

They go to church every Sunday. He in hand-me-down suit. A tie. He likes dress-up. Likes church. Catholic mass. The ceremony. The music. The smell of incense. The comfort of ritual. He participates. Likes the belonging. Sings along. Takes the wafer. A bigger family.

The Saenz treat him well. But not family. Watches Saenz boys. Act like brothers. Tease, fight, play. Just like in the books. He wants that. Never says anything. Tries once. Tease, challenge. The boys gang up on him. Not a bad beating. Had worse from Crewcut. Never tries again. Outside the family. Always outside.

In the Spring head north. Kids out of school month early.

Start school month late. Follow the green season. Strawberries, cherries, blue berries, seven cents a pound. Then orchards. Apples, peaches pears. Hard work. Hauling ladders from tree to tree, from fruit laden branch to laden branch. Bag filled until too heavy. Dumped into crates, bushels. The whole family works. Kids chided to produce.

Sunrise to sundown. Long days. Sunburn. Fields sprayed while working. Insecticide. Everyone holds breath. Handkerchiefs and t-shirts over mouth.

Live in shacks. Tin roofed. Cement block walls. Unpainted. No plumbing. Outhouses. Sundays off. Religious farmers forbid Sabbath breakage. Rich farmers. Big white houses. Sons with fancy cars.

Sundays go to town. Maybe see a movie. Popcorn and candy allowance. Sees strawberry picking girl with boy. Know her name now. Irena. Older guy. Man. Arturo.

Some Sunday nights there's music. Men play guitars. An accordion. Singing. Sad songs. Dancing. Arturo dances with Irena. Close.

Billy follows Arturo to shithouse. Waits with two-by-four. Decides Irena at fault. Lets Arturo go.

Sometimes trouble with other boys. Name calling. White boy bullshit. Has to fight. Fights hard. Sometimes beaten. Never quits. Knocked down. Bloodied. Hits back. Gets up crazy. Has to be beaten unconscious. Word gets around. Loco gringo. Most leave him alone. Not all.

In late summer work the muck farms. River bottom lands. Lettuce, celery, carrots. Bent over all day.

Billy works hard. Wants them to keep him around.

* * *

Christmas. Big tree. Cut themselves. Stolen from the woods. Or tree farm. Lots of decorations. Lots of presents. One for Billy.

Family dinners. Noisy. Everybody talks. Not Billy. Outside the conversations. Outside. Always outside.

Ignored at school. Didn't know anything about anything. Sits in classes. Ignorant. Sits in the back. Quiet. Fine with most teachers.

One takes interest. Mrs. Hamilton. Teaches him to read. Doesn't know why she singles him out. Just does.

Not nice woman. Not mean. Strict. Not soft hearted. Armor around her heart. Teaches him day after day. Every school day. All year. Billy catches on quick.

One day she stops. You don't need me anymore. He did. Didn't cry. Wanted to. Should have thanked her.

Library is sanctuary. Hours upon hours alone there. Reads fast. Devours books. At school. In room. Always has a book. Saenz boys mock. Don't push him though. Has reputation now. Will fight.

Likes library best. Cool in the summer. Warm in the winter. Quiet. Nobody bothers him. Surrenders to the lives of others.

* * *

1960. Quick fingers fly. Strawberries plucked. Ripe only. Leave the green. Leave the white. Billy crawls along the row. Long hair in his eyes. A ruthless sun. Sweat runs in rivers. Down neck. Down back. Down brow into eyes. Stings.

Saenz all pick. Adults. Kids. No excuses.

Oscar, middle boy. Picks next row.

Opposite side a Mexican girl. Same age as Billy. Wears man's shirt. Too big for her. She bends over berry plants. No bra. Breasts revealed. Little pointed titties. Mostly nipple. Still forming.

Billy transfixed. Girl catches him looking.

Billy embarrassed. Blushes hot. Focuses on fruit.

Girl smiles at him. Billy sees it.

"That's eatin' pussy." Oscar snorts. His laugh. Oscar is twelve. Dirty words still amuse him.

"I think she likes me," Billy whispers to him. Statement or hope? Billy doesn't know.

Oscar snorts louder. Billy empties bucket into crate. Crate sectioned into pints. Goes back to picking. Sneaks another look at girl.

She's gone. His heart falls.

A tap on his shoulder. It's her. Heart sails.

"Your name Billy."

"Yeah."

"I see something. In trees."

She points to woods. Nearby. Borders strawberry fields.

"What? A possum?"

He saw possum in woods last night. Luminous devil eyes. Rat tail.

She just smiles. Half smile. Walks into woods. Billy follows. Into the forest. Thick with trees. Pines and hardwoods. The field disappears.

"What'd it look like? Silver gray like? With a rat's tail?"

"Over here."

His eyes follow. Jet black hair. Skintight jeans. She sits under a big pine. Bed of brown needles.

He stands above her. Explores her face. Madonna. Like in the pictures at church, in books.

She takes off the shirt. Pale skin. Dark nipples. Lays the shirt down. Eases back onto it. Wiggles out of her jeans. A sinuous dance. White panties. They glow.

She smiles at him.

"You can kiss me. Only one time. If you want."

Want?

Billy kneels before her. Like in church.

Oscar had a skin mag. Pages wrinkled, curled, crispy. No cover. Always hidden. Like treasure. Not just titties. Bush. Twat treasure. Asked Billy once.

"Ever seen Bush?"

"Yeah."

"Bullshit."

Billy remembers Crewcut's whores. Sluts and slatterns. Hairy cunts. Red and purple pussy flesh. Wet pussy. Matted hair. Hair crawling to belly button. Hair creeping down thighs.

"Ain't seen twat since your mamas," Oscar sneered.

Billy shrugs. Lets it go. Likes Oscar. Oscar is the middle child. Between two boys. Older Enrico, a.k.a. Ricky Junior, and Ramon. Two girls, both younger. Veronica, a.k.a. Ronnie and Fanny. Boys are handsome. Girls are beautiful. Fine pale skin. Spanish blood Mama Saenz says. Castilian. Proud. Great hair. Handsome jaw. Tall. Thin.

Oscar is squat. Dark skin. Pimples. Family calls him "Monstro." Monster. Joking. Not funny.

Parents fawn over other kids. Sunday dress up. Church people fawn over Saenz kids. Comments on their beauty. Oscar and Billy watch.

Billy walks out of woods. Back to his row. His bucket. His crate. Strawberries. Dick still wet in pants. Back to picking.

Oscar comes over. Offers jug. Kool-Aid. Warm from sun. Sweet.

Oscar grins.

"Whatcha been doin' in the woods?"

Billy silent. Still processing.

"Huh? Huh? Huh? Huh?"

"She saw something. A critter. I think."

"Did you see it? Bet it was a beaver."

Oscar giggles. Like a girl.

"I think she likes me."

"Sure she does."

Billy's face hot. With anger. Glares at Oscar.

"I know she likes me."

Oscar steps back.

Billy looks to girl. She rises from her own row. Walks toward

Billy. Bends down. Glimpse of titties again. She takes Billy's crate. Mostly full. Takes it to her row.

"Hey!" Billy cries out. She smiles. He doesn't.

Billy gets it. Oh.

Oscar looks at Billy. Sad for him.

Billy's hurt shows. Only a moment. Sets his jaw. "Don't be a pussy," echoes from somewhere. Grits his teeth against the pain. In his heart. His chest.

Okay.

*  *  *

Green season over. Billy lives with Saenz family. In his pantry room. School and night work. Late fall and winter, early spring. Janitorial services. Cleaning offices. Kids work until midnight school nights. Mama and Papa Saenz 'til three in the morning. Then their day jobs.

Billy mops floors. Scrubs toilets. Saenz kids work. Ronnie lazy. Boys steal things. Little things. From desks. Candy. Coins. Fancy pens for school. Rules; never take it all. Just some.

Steal food from fridges.

One day janitorial jobber Mrs. Ramirez asks Mama Saenz, "The blue eyes?"

"Someone died," Mama Saenz says. "He has no one else."

# CHAPTER FOUR

Junior steals cars. Drives them south. Across border. Steal them at night. By morning the car's in Mexico. Gone forever. Sometimes Oscar follows in Junior's car.

Drives him back home. Billy goes with.

Big cars. Cadillacs. Olds 98. Buick 225. Luxury riding. Smooth shocks. The cars float through the night. Electric windows. AC. Border radio stations. Rock'n'roll and Tex-Mex music.

Good times in Nuevo Laredo. Bars and whorehouses. Junior did drugs. Marijuana.

Coke. Oscar learned to drink. Great student. Tequila. Ate the worm. Junior got stupid when high. Oscar got mean when drunk. Picked fights. With everybody.

Mean then stupid. Billy abstained. No drugs. No booze. Stupid got you into trouble.

Mean and stupid got you in big trouble. Junior spent some time in jail. Oscar too.

Billy stayed clean.

* * *

Spring. Strawberry crop failed. Too much rain. Cherries and blueberries late. Oscar and Billy take a job at the country club. Fort Sam Houston. Military types. Ground maintenance. Golf course. Caddy the players when course busy. Extra money in tips. Billy still gives it all to Mama Saenz.

Painting lines on tennis courts. Woman sees Billy. His tight pants. His long hair. She doesn't know. Pants tight 'cause can't afford new jeans. Growing fast. Long hair not a rebellion. No James Dean, Marlon Brando here. Just poor boy. Can't afford haircuts every week. Fanny cuts his hair.

Not sexy. Just poor.

Military wives. Husbands overseas. Bored. Horny.

Mrs. Glaser passes him to Mrs. Bluth. Who passes him to Mrs. Teener. Passes around like they traded tennis rackets. Okay with Billy. Sex and some money. They always gave him money. 'Cause he looked like he needed it? Guilt?

Seventeen. Slim and wiry. Greases hair. Pompadour ala Junior. Teachers harass. Too long in back. Duck ass. Sideburns. Tight ass pants. Attitude walk. Hoodlum. Juvenile delinquent. Rich kids sneer. Don't fuck with. Billy fights. Crazy when angry. Gets a rep. It has to be tested occasionally. Okay with him.

Motel room. The Alamo Lies. What does that mean? No one knows. On the highway. Vacancies. Shag carpet. Smells of cigarettes. Bed. TV. Bureau. Paintings screwed to wall. Like anybody would want to steal them.

Washes dick in sink. Zips up. Black Levi's. Tight as paint. Adjust balls. Black cowboy shirt. Pearl snap buttons. Pointed toed boots. Mexican fence climbers.

Woman in bed. Wiggling into girdle. Forties. Black hair. Dyed. Bush brown. Flesh bulges, top of girdle. Top of legs.

"You make love like you're mad at me."

"I don't make love. I fuck."

Combs hair in mirror. Carefully loops curl over forehead. Turns up dollar in back. Very Elvis.

"I know, sweet William. I know. You fuck delightfully."

"Don't call me that."

Black bra. She leans forward. Drops tit into cups. Like bread dough into pan. Plop. Pendulous tits.

"You're mad at me."

Fastens bra. Enters bathroom. Billy switches on TV. Doesn't like sound of douching. Reclines on bed. Looks at shoes. Cuban heels worn down. Soles thin. Can feel gravel underfoot when walking. Needs new pair.

"You promised me a job."

"I said I'd do my best." Her voice full of bathroom reverb. Tub faucet running. Filling bag.

TV needs to warm up. Jack Bailey shouts. Gonna make some lucky woman "Queen For A Day!"

"I want a regular job. For the summer. Nine-to-five. Talk to your husband."

"I said I'm working on it."

"He gives all those jerkoffs at school summer jobs. All those college assholes."

"Roland considers that a service to the community. Besides, those boys are sons of his friends. He has an obligation."

She comes out of the bathroom. Snapping on earrings. Hair fixed. "Anyway, he won't hire any spics."

Sees something in his eyes.

"Now, I know you're not one of them, darling. But you live with them. You congregate with them."

Billy silent. Congregate, shit. Stares at ceiling. Jaw clenched.

"Personally, I don't give a hoot. My people have always been democrats. But Roland..."

Billy glances at TV. Pays attention. "I'll be a sonofabitch."

President is dead. Kennedy. Dallas. Shot.

Woman is mid dress.

"What?"

"Somebody shot Kennedy. He's dead."

She plops on bed. Stares at TV. Billy thinks of Mama Saenz.

Two pictures in living room. The Pope and Kennedy. Both hand-tinted. Soft colors. Pink faces. Rosy cheeks.

"Marlene's gonna die. She's just gonna die." Woman stares at the screen. Gasps. Jackie Kennedy gets on a plane. People crying. News announcer crying.

Billy could give a shit. It don't affect him. His life. Why they crying for him? Anger seeping into Billy's brain.

"Roland's gonna be looking for me. I gotta run."

She rises. Grabs purse. Looks around. Stuffs nylons into purse. Billy stands. Between her and door.

"I need some money."

"Oh, I'm a little short right now, darlin'. Next time."

"Now."

"No." A whine. Offended.

Slap. Billy hits top of her head. Stiff sprayed hair. Like slapping a Brillo pad.

"Listen you old cunt. It's bad enough I got to fuck you. But I ain't going away with nothing. You can't get me no job, I want cash. Cough it up."

Tears in her eyes. Hand to head. Adjusts her 'do.

"Don't be mean."

"Don't be mean? Jesus, what do I have to do for a decent job around here? Fuck old Roland?"

Grabs her purse.

"Whataya got here? Any 'pin' money? What's fucking 'pin' money anyway? You buy a lot of fucking pins? Anything in here for 'sweet William'?"

Dumps purse contents. Onto bed. She reaches for them. Billy raises his hand. A warning. She backs off.

He grabs bills. Rifles wallet. Takes car keys.

"This'll do. And I'm borrowing your car."

Leaves room. Slams door. Woman sits on bed. Cries. Wails at TV.

Outside. Blistering heat. Her car. Corvette. Beauty. Throaty engine roar. Rooster tail of gravel. Tiny rocks rain on motel door.

Billy cruises. Top down. Radio full blast. Washed this car. Hundreds of others. Part time at Roland's dealership.

Rolls past golf course. Oscar mowing grass. Billy honks. Waves. Goodbye.

No one else for goodbye. Junior married. Kid on the way. Miserable. Drinks all the time. Ramon in jail. Burgled gas station. Billy with him. Ramon caught selling Valvoline. Billy got away. Ronnie pregnant at fifteen. Getting fat. Father Saenz with cancer. Lungs. Mother Saenz mourns. Prays all the time. Blames Billy for Ramon. Ramon was burglary ringleader. Billy doesn't tell her. Takes blame. To make her happy. Less unhappy.

Nothing to keep him here. No possessions. Nothing.

Heads south.

# CHAPTER FIVE

Joined the Army. Not joined. Given an either or. One side of the equation—jail. DA suggestion. On draft board. Every 'miscreant' enlisted equals one 'good boy' allowed to 'go on with his life.'

Billy had to look up 'miscreant.' Didn't bother looking up 'good boy.' Meant rich kid. Desperate recruiter recruited by judge. Patriots all. Off to basic training.

Immediate attitude problem. CO calls it 'authority figure problem.' College graduate. Billy fights. With other recruits. Squad leader. Platoon sergeant. Drill Instructor. Still, they don't kick him out. Need bodies. Move him on.

Advanced Infantry Training. A lot of marching. Classes; Oral Hygiene, Chain of Command, Sex Hygiene. In hot rooms. Nodding off.

Marksmanship. M-14 rifle, M-60 machine gun, .45 1911A1 pistol, BAR. Billy excels. Expert badge.

Tactics. Squad movement. Platoon.

Bayonet. Kill! Kill! Kill! Billy excels. Like dancing but with menace. Deadly menace. Billy more aggressive than most boys.

Still more fights. Other recruits. Instructors. Platoon

Sergeant. Lose some. Lose most. But learning. Sergeant Sadler takes Billy aside. Tries to make a soldier.

"Call me Larry." Everyone calls him 'Barry.' 'Cause of the song, "Ballad of the Green Berets." Says Billy has potential. Billy studies manuals. Gets promoted. Billy transferred at end of training. No more Larry.

Only recruit in Basic Training who never gets a letter at mail call. Advanced Infantry Training, same deal. The only soldier not to get a letter. Jump School. No letters. Assigned to the 101$^{st}$ Airborne, Fort Campbell, Kentucky. No mail.

Billy bored. Same shit. Over and over. Oral hygiene again. Weapon maintenance. More fights. Ignorant redneck NCO's telling him what to do. Lieutenant tells him to pick up cigarette butt.

"I don't smoke, sir."

"Nobody asked you. Pick it up, soldier."

"Fuck you."

Stockade.

Cold. Winter. No snow. Patches of ice. Frozen mud. Two story wood barracks. Old World War leftover housing. Surrounded by chain link fence. The whole place surrounded by two more fences. Dog run in between. All fences topped with barbed wire. Now called razor wire. Guard towers like wooden giants glaring down at prisoners.

Crowded. Army grabbing every swinging dick off the streets. Cannon fodder draft. Some have a prison habit.

Bunks inches apart, two high. Men, some boys. Smoke and joke. Card games. Water hearts. Cigarettes as money. No books. Library on lock down. Stabbing.

Billy trades. Cigarette issue for candy. Candy traded to guards for contraband books. Reads same books over and over. Lost in the words.

Barracks segregated. Blacks upstairs. By choice or policy? Tension. Race riots in the cities. Black power. Revolution. Redneck backlash. Blacks aren't Billy's problem.

Billy goes to latrine. Long room. Eight toilets on one side. Eight sinks on the other side. With mirrors. Old but clean. Army inspection clean. Shower at far end.

Billy walks to shower. Occupied. Loves his showers. With Saenz family bathed once a week. Bathtub. Water re-used. Billy at tail end of use. Army showers every day, twice a day. The ultimate luxury. Billy loves his showers.

This time shower occupied. Seven men in corner. Circle another man. Boy. On his knees.

"Suck motherfucker."

"Like it was a Tootsie Roll Pop."

"Put a lip lock on that love muscle, sweet thang." Laughs.

"Know what you get when you put a nickel in a hippie's ear? His teeth roll back and hair grows on his lips."

Laughs. A slap.

"No teeth. Watch it, ya little bitch."

"You might want to knock those teeth out, for the future, you know."

"You want some peace motherfucker? Here's a piece. Piece of my tube steak."

"Bet he had long hair he looked just like a girl."

Everybody's hair shaved. Makes boy on his knees look eight years old. Crying. Nose running. Bruise on cheek. Hands hang limp.

Boy's ear grabbed, yanked into another crotch. Billy watches. "What you looking at cocksucker?"

"We got us another pussy?"

"Hey, punk, you brought your kneepads?"

Four move toward Billy. MP guard outside latrine. Looks the other way.

"Don't fuck with me." Billy warns.

"Relax. We're not going to fuck with you. We're going to fuck you."

"Or fuck you up."

"Let's cornhole the cocksucker."

Billy steps into them. Never retreat from a threat. Speaks softly.

"You motherfuckers might kick the shit outa me. There's four of you. Maybe more. But I'm gonna kill one of you. If I have to rip out your throat with my teeth. I'm gonna blind one of you. If I have to claw out your eyeball with my bare hands. One of you I'm gonna rip your balls off. And if I don't do it now, I do it later. Some day. Some how. So…you're gonna have to kill me. Now. If you can."

They look at each other. The leader checks out the others. They don't look confident.

"So, is it worth it. You can get away fucking up some punk. But killing a fella? The MP's can't have that on their watch. So think about it."

"Damn, Jim, you think you're one bad motherfucker."

The leader steps back. One step. Billy quiet.

"Hey, man, no offense. Just woof talk. You know how it is."

"Yeah, I know how it is." Billy walks to urinal. Pisses. Hears slapping noise behind him.

"Who's next?"

The four return to the gang-bang. Billy shuts it out. Walks out.

* * *

Billy works the circle jerk. At one end concrete mixed. Poured. Forms broken. Slab, two-by-two-by-four feet. Hauled to other end of stockade. Prisoners with sledgehammers pound slab into gravel. Gravel hauled to pour site. Made into new slab. Billy carts slabs with dolly. Hauls gravel in wheelbarrow back.

All day. Every day. Busy work. Idle hands are the devil's workshop. The circle jerk makes Billy crazy. It haunts him.

* * *

Billy sleeps light. Blanket parties. Throw blanket over victim in bed. Beat with steel bed extensions. One every week. Punks. Hippies. Draft dodgers. Fresh meat.

Billy wakes to screams. Breaking glass. Scans barracks. No movement. More screams. Outside. Others wake. Billy goes to window.

MP tangled in the razor wire. Top of fence. Upstairs guard. More glass shatters. Beds fly out upper windows. Mattresses follow. Klaxon blares. Tower lights pop on. Glare pans fences, barracks.

Other barracks follow. Blacks raging. Guards beaten. Whites attacked. Killings promised through shouts.

Standoff in Billy's barracks. Whites arm themselves. Bed extensions. Soap in socks. Razors. Shivs. Stalemate between upstairs and down.

Infantry surround stockade. New M-16s. M-60s. Jeep mounted fifties. Armored unit.

Fire trucks arrive. Turn hoses on barracks. Blow out windows remaining. Flood interiors. Drench prisoners.

No food. No heat. Two days. Two nights. Cold days. Colder nights.

Beatings. Fights. Prisoner against prisoner.

Overnight freeze. Billy shivering. Blacks quiet. Rage dissipated. Blacks surrender at first light.

Prisoners ordered outside. Ordered to strip. Ordered into yard. Into prone position. Billy face down. On ice. Frozen mud. Toes numb. Thighs and chest numb. Dick numb. Numbness turns into pain. Shivering. Teeth chattering.

Taken away. One at a time.

"Take me! Take me! Take me!" Prisoners volunteer. Led away. MPs with shotguns and M -16s.

"What the fuck happened?"

Guards cut no slack. Billy prodded with butt of gun.

"Martin Luther King killed."

Black prisoner beaten. Singled out. No protest. Expected

retaliation.

"Murdered."

Guards get their revenge. Billy clubbed with gun butt. "Assassinated is what it was."

Some prisoners carried out on stretchers.

Billy doesn't care. Martin Luther King. Big deal. Doesn't affect him. Prison does.

* * *

Off limits library. Used to meet counsel. Billy eyes books. Hungry for books. Billy's lawyer. Black Second Lieutenant. Green. OCS fresh meat.

"Who was this Martin Luther King?" Billy asks.

"A great man."

"Like them Kennedys?" Billy doesn't care. Small talk.

"Maybe greater."

Billy shrugs.

"You don't buy that?"

"What'd he ever do for me."

Green lieutenant gets the message. Opens file. "Let's talk about your court-martial."

"Yeah, let's do that. What's going down here?"

"Well, I don't really know." Green lieutenant embarrassed. "This is my first time at this kind of thing."

First time. Billy nods. Fuck me.

"Yeah, but you're a lawyer. You know these things. What they gonna do to me?"

"I'm not a lawyer. Just a lieutenant from the Signal Corps. Every officer has to participate in a court-martial. You know, to be eligible for promotion. I...uh..."

Billy gets it. Army's different. Has its own ways. Billy's still learning. How this system works. Smiles at the lieutenant.

"It was your turn in the barrel."

Green lieutenant nods.

"Just punching your ticket."

Another nod. "Affirmative."

Fuck. Goddamned cherry lieutenant. Goddamned virgin lawyer. I am so fucked.

Billy contemplates the racks of books they won't let him read. Off limits. Story of his life.

Leans into lawyer. Lawyer shrinks back.

"Do you know what it's like in here?' These hippie kids, protesting the war, the draft? They get sent here. Full of peace and love and shit. They won't fight. In the war. They get thrown in here with hardcore cons. Then they get eaten alive. "

Green lieutenant has no clue. None.

"Listen." Billy tries for eye contact. "I want out of here. Make some kind of fucking deal. There's always a deal to be made. See what they'll give me if I cop a plea. Save 'em a trial. Court-martial. I want out."

"There may be a way."

# CHAPTER SIX

Viet Nam. Eleven Bravo. Infantryman. Ground pounder. Grunt. Fresh meat. Billy finds his place.

Charges that hill. Survives. Another hill. Survives again. Good at survival. Promoted. Busted to Private E1 back in states. Makes PFC on a hill. One of fourteen left after assault. Started with full company. One hundred forty men - boys. Fourteen left. All men now. The rest dead or wounded. Gone on helicopters.

Another company formed. Full reinforced company. One hundred sixty men, plus. Up another hill. Billy makes rank by attrition. SpecFour. Then Sergeant. Good at this.

In the middle of a firefight. Blood and mud. Screams and gunfire. Radioman runs up to Billy. "We landed on the moon!" Means nothing to Billy. Radioman takes a round in the back. Can't feel his legs. Gone on another chopper.

Billy is good at survival. Better at killing. Kills with efficiency. With M-16. With grenades. With his hands.

Billy gets mail. Random females, high school students and college girls and religious types write anonymous soldiers in Nam. Supporting the troops. Billy writes eighteen-year-old Chrissy back. Another letter arrives. Billy's imagination takes flight. Creates a family back home. Home being Bowling Green,

Ohio. Likes the sound of it. Everly Brothers song. Billy creates a brother, younger. Makes up a life, a family. Part Hardy Boys, part Ozzie and Harriet. Brother sings in a band. Chrissy never questions. Sends a photo. Pretty girl. With glasses. All American girl. Clairol girl - with glasses. Make plans to meet after Nam. Her letters get religious. Sends him a Bible. He stops writing. Keeps picture. In wallet. In waterproof bag. Black-and-white photo cracks like old porcelain. Billy occasionally looks at it. Remembers his fake family. Their fictive future. It comforts him. Until it hurts. Then he puts photo away.

Stays in Nam. Extends tour. Once. Twice. First time as infantry. The next as Recon. Billy does even better in Recon. Out in the boonies with small team. No ignorant officer ordering him to 'charge that hill.' Picks his men. Picks his missions. Brings back good intel. Kills the NVA officers for CYA.

But not really a team player. Allowed to go out alone. One-man patrols. Excels. Signs up for third tour.

Recruited by Spooks. CIA. They don't admit it. Wear fatigues with no name patch. No U.S. Army patch. Carry Beretta in shoulder holster. No Army issue .45 on hip. 'Who the fuck are you' mystery men. But everybody knows.

Grab Billy. Assigned to Phoenix Program.

"What the fuck is a Phoenix Program?"

* * *

Village incursion. Night. A few dozen huts. Nothing moves. First the dogs. Dogs are a threat. Sniff out intruder. Bark. Alert the village.

Billy kills a monkey. On the trail in. Shot with silenced CAR-15. Carbine version of M-16. Eighteen inches of silencer.

Spider monkey in a tree. Glowering at Billy. .223 round tears monkey in half.

Village perimeter. Monkey carcass attached to nylon parachute cord. Body tossed into village. Dog snort it out. Little mongrel dog. Approaches with trepidation. Good reason. Become food themselves in tough times. Growls low in throat. Grabs monkey meat. Jaws clamp down. Trots off. Cord stops. Tied to Billy's foot.

Billy takes out wrist rocket. Unfolds aluminum frame slingshot. Mail order from states. Ball bearings in pocket. Embedded in paraffin to prevent rattling. Pries one out. Puts in pad. Pulls back surgical tubing. Aims. Fifteen feet.

Dog pulling at monkey meat. Billy lets loose. Thunk. Dog falls. Tiny yelp. Back legs kicking at dirt. Ball bearing stuck in forehead. Glinting in moonlight. Third eye.

No sound. Slingshot silent. Effective. Even with men. Silenced CAR cough too much noise at night.

Cuts dog's throat. Just in case. Waits. No other dogs. Watched village for two days. From tree line. Counted only one dog. But it pays to be sure. Village poor.

Re-pockets wrist rocket.

Nothing moves in village.

Slow crawls to nearest hut. Pulls out map. Made during two-day surveillance. Moves slow. Quiet. Flashlight. Red filter. Wraps fingers around lens. Flicks on. Leaks light through fingers. Examines map. Layout of village. Three huts marked with 'x.' And names. Truong, Duyet, Nguyen. Didn't need names.

Checks village. Notes three designated huts. Puts map away.

Inside a hut. Five people sleep. Mats on dirt floor. Billy creeps among them. Examining faces in moonlight. Old woman. Young woman. Kids.

Crouches over man. Pulls photo. Black and white. Blow up from long distance. Given by Spooks. Same man. Truong.

Billy pockets photo. Pulls knife from leg sheath. Metal whispers against leather. Gerber commando knife. Laminated blade. Sharp. Traded captured SKS for it.

Billy slides hand over Truong's mouth. Man's eyes pop open. Press Gerber against chest. Between third and fourth rib.

Billy puts all his weight behind blade. Slides past bone. Jerks blade right to left. Cuts heart in half.

Truong goes limp. Instantly. Billy pulls blade free. Lays knife in crook of Truong's arm. Folds dead arm closed around blade. Pulls it through, past pajama sleeve. Clean.

Second man's hut. Movement. Billy ducks into deep black shadows. Man exits hut. Walks to edge of clearing. At green line. Pulls up leg of baggy black pajama trousers. Urinates. Billy waits.

Man squats. Lights cigarette. Enjoys a smoke. Billy checks his photos. Pisser is Nguyen.

Billy creeps around. Behind Nguyen. One cautious foot in front of another. Eyes find spot to place each foot. Ease down toe, heel, toe, heel.

Two meters behind Nguyen. Billy waits. Like a stone.

Nguyen contemplates cigarette ember.

Two quick steps. One arm over man's head. Four fingers into Nguyen's mouth. Feel upper teeth. Against fingers. Yank head up. Bares the neck. Other hand slices throat with Gerber. Queer gasp from opened windpipe. Nguyen thrashes. Blood spurts. Both Jugulars. Seconds seem forever. Body goes slack.

Billy double checks for life. None there. Steamy vapor rises from cut throat. Wipe blade in crook of arm. Somewhere in the village a baby whimpers.

Billy moves to third hut.

In. Confirm. Kill.

Wipes blade for third time. Hears stifled cry. Turns. Woman cowers in darkness. White of her eyes bright. Two quick steps. Slaps hand over her mouth. Stabs, jerks blade. Woman trembles for a second. Then is still.

Shadow in the doorway. Billy whirls.

A little boy. Backlit by moonlight.

Billy rises. Slow like smoke. Mesmerized by boy's shadow. Slow motion walks to entrance.

Boy's shadow disappears. Was it real?

Billy walks across village. Searching. But not seeing boy. Confused. Lost. Fugue state. Not knowing why.

Drops knife. Steel slips from unfeeling fingers.

Behind Billy. Boy scurries across village clearing. Bloody knife glints in moonlight. Boy picks it up.

Looks for man. Sees him disappear into jungle. Black shadows of tree line suck the man in.

# CHAPTER SEVEN

Big noise. Noise so loud. Cuts through your skin. Pounds your bones. Rumble and hum. Lathes whine. Ten ton presses quake the floor. Air compressors hiss. Clatter and clamor, steel on steel. Continuous cacophonous din.

Billy in a factory. Dirt and oil everywhere. Floor caked with oil, metal shavings and dust. Billy drives a forklift. Once bright yellow. Now, dull, battered. Scraped and dented. Been through a war.

Billy long haired. Mustache. Doing third shift. Graveyard shift. Totes a steel box. Loaded with raw steel. Flanges. Weaves between drill presses. Drops box off. Toots horn.

Carts empty away. Hauls full boxes of drilled parts. Stacks. Back and forth. All night. Feeding machines and men. Parts drilled, bent, welded, molded, turned, cut and bored. Men part of the machines. Jerking handles. Slamming buttons. Feeding jaws of press. Feeding drill, lathe and punch.

Billy stops. Horizontal torch cutter. Set electric light onto blueprint. Eye follows the pattern. Acetylene torch cuts the steel accordingly. Inch thick steel. Billy likes to watch torch. Burning bright with power. Melting steel. Sputtering and sparking.

Torch following its path. Like the people who work here. Their eyes locked on a pattern. Pattern their lives will follow. Cutting through the days and nights without variance. He could do this.

Old man monitors cutter. Asleep on stool. Chin on chest.

Billy raps pipe onto forklift roll bar. Clang, clang, clang.

"Wake up ya old fart!" Billy yells over the manufacturing noise. "Wake up and piss, the world's on fire!"

Old man wakes with a start. Scowls at Billy. Wipes drool from bristled chin. Checks torch.

"Fuck you." He growls. Billy laughs.

Silas. Big man. Over six feet. Big gut. Bear of a man. Old though. Broad shoulders now slumping. Back bent from sixty years of burden. Skin brownish black. Hair gray and white. Eyes yellow, watery.

Silas grabs tongs, gloves. Pries cut part from rollers. Edges still glow red. Silas hammers off slag. Throws part into box. Pulls steel slab across rollers. Aligns torch. Starts electric eye across blue line again. Torch pops and sputters. Slices through steel. Molten slag spurts under. Fourth of July sparklers.

Silas adjust his flame.

Billy watches the ritual. Silas done this how many thousand times? A million?

Silas gives Billy the finger. Billy laughs. Silas pours himself a cup. Thermos of Irish coffee. More Irish than coffee. Winces. Perches back on stool. Closes eyes. Nods off.

Billy goes back to runs.

* * *

Billy and Silas in a boat. Small outboard. Silas takes a lot of space. Billy not so much. Summer calm lake. Fishing. Silas drinks beer. Cooler at his feet. Two six packs of Bud. Billy drinks Dr Pepper. Liter bottle in the cooler.

Fish all day. Silent. Neither talks much. Watching their

bobbers. Both comfortable with the silence. Conversation unnecessary. Sit like this for hours.

"Lunch?" Silas asks. Doesn't need, want an answer. Billy tosses the old man a paper sack. Hostess cupcakes. Chocolate. Unwraps cellophane. Tosses one to Billy. Both scarf them. Two bags of potato chips. Barbecue. One each.

Ring of Baloney. Silas cuts off chunk with bait knife. Tosses it to Billy. Cuts one for self.

Eat in silence. Water laps at boat. Bobbing with soft swells. Finished, Silas dumps his chip dust into lake. Dips fingers. Wipes face. Wipes big old wrinkled hands on overalls.

"Like to catch me some bluegills." Silas mumbles. "Tired a perch. Used to be lots of bluegills here."

Scratches chin stubble. His ass. His head. Hours go by.

One day.

"My daughter writ me," Silas says. No prompting. Maybe talking to himself. Hard to tell. Does that. "Married again. Says she lives in Georgia now."

Billy doesn't comment. Doesn't know if he is supposed to.

"I tol' you 'bout her?" Silas is talking to him."

"Yeah." Billy nods. "Said she was a whore."

"A cheap hoor." Silas laughs. "Asked me for money. Wants me to send it to Georgia. By telegram. Onliest time in seven years she writ me. She asts me for money. No how-de-do. Jack shit. Money. Gimme, gimme."

Silas pauses. Scratches some more. A little embarrassed. So many words at once. Personal words.

"I wonder what happened to all the bluegills?"

"You musta caught them all."

Silas laughs. "Musta. And et 'em all too."

Billy laughs. They fish until the after noon. Go home. Sleep until work.

That's his summer. Get off at seven a.m.. Stop at the liquor store. Booze and soda. Something to fill the gut.

Fish and think. Viet Nam fills his head. Not scary thoughts. Thoughts about That Kid. The one in the village. What became of the boy? What is he doing now? Alive? Fighting? Which side. Billy knows.

After the village Billy quit the field. Quit the Program. Army quits on him. Discharged. Fort Lewis. Offered plane ticket home. Where's home? Stays in Washington. Winds up in Spokane.

* * *

Billy rents a house. Hates apartments. Too many people. Too close. Finds old Victorian cheap. Peeling paint. Dirty windows. Buys a sofa. A table. Two matching chairs. Piles of book everywhere. A little television. Red plastic bean bag chair in front of the stereo.

Japanese sound system. Turntable. Records. Big ass speakers. Led Zeppelin loud. "Super Session", Al Cooper, Mike Bloomfield, Stephen Stills. Over and over. "It Takes A Lot To Laugh, It Takes A Train To Cry", "Season Of The Witch". Over and over.

Eats out of bags. McDonalds is his lunch bucket. Fridge full of soda. Mountain Dew. Dr Pepper. Coke. Hates Pepsi.

Leaves tv on 24/7. Sound low. Constant murmur of voices. Company but won't admit it.

Washes clothes once a week. No bedding. Sleeps on sofa. Army surplus poncho liner for a blanket.

Buys a car. '70 Mustang. Mach One. Muscle car.

Buys a motorcycle. Triumph Triton twin cylinder in a Norton featherbed frame. Foreign bike. Need metric tools. Pain in the ass. But fuck that 'buy American' bullshit.

Like to cruise back roads at night on weekends. All alone in the world. Face in the wind. Headlight carving out a tunnel ahead.

Brings nobody to the house. Lives alone. Trying to figure things out. Life. His life. Where does he fit in?

He can do this. Become a citizen. Millions of people do it every day. He can do this.

* * *

Boring job. Boring fishing. Boredom is what he wants. When you're bored you think. He needs to think.

Everybody at work bitches. The job. The wife. The kids. Their cars. Their lives.

Billy complains about nothing.

Punches in at eleven. Stands in line. Punch clock slams his time card. Bites in the time.

In line behind Silas. Old man dumps half of thermos onto parking lot. Replaces with Johnny Walker. Winks at Billy.

"It's a world of hurt but I gots plenty of anesthesia."

* * *

Billy rolls from machine to machine. Raw stock in yard. Outside in the fresh air. Inside to the stink of grease and ozone. Finished parts to loading dock.

Back to machines. A man screams. Falls to floor. Clutching mangled hand. Blood and torn meat and splintered white bone. Billy hops of hi-lo. Tourniquets. Good at first-aid. Had lots of practice. Worse shit than this.

Everybody freaking out.

"Don't look," Billy tells him. "Don't look." Uses ballpoint pen to twist tourniquet tight. Other men gather around. Injured man looks. Stupid fuck. Screams. Faints.

Two men push through crowd with stretcher. Another rushes over with white first-aid kit. Pushes Billy aside.

"Whatcha think you're doin'? I'm the first-aid designate on this shift."

Billy ignores him. Walks back to his Chalmers. Likes the smell of propane leading from tank. Drives away. Half-ton press keeps pounding on puddle of blood. Red splashing.

Billy rolls to the back. Silas with chin on chest. Torch cutting away at nothing. At end of track.

"Half-ton safety blew. Ate Meister's hand."

No response from Silas. Billy beats a ball-peen hammer against the roll bar.

"Wake up ya old goat!"

Still nothing.

Billy climbs down. Walks over knowing. Crouches down in front of Silas. Silas mouth open. Thread of spittle hangs to chest. Eyes wide open. Seeing nothing.

Billy knows dead when he sees it. Knows dead better than most.

Stands staring at dead Silas. Blinks a few times. Tears come anyway. Turns away. Stares at cutter. Torch still burns. Billy kicks machine.

Not enough. Rips up blueprint. Shreds it. Tosses under torch. Flares up. Burns.

Stares at the dead old man. Is that me? In thirty years? An old drunk. Dying at his machine. To be replaced like a spare part? Is this me? What I want to be?

* * *

Memorial at the Skyline Bar. Factory hangout after shift. Billy rarely goes. Others give him the gotch eye when he orders only soda.

Goes this time. Evident nobody knows Silas well. Just an excuse for toasts. Memorial soon becomes just another morning. Booze, bullshit and bumper pool. Delaying going home. They leave, one, two at a time. Half dozen left.

Silas…twenty-seven years on the line. Shitty way to go. Old drunk. But still…

Shitty way to go.

Sign near cash register. "Gun for sale. Model '94 Winshester. Best offer." Billy stands at bar. Orders Seven Up. Bartender puts cherry in soda.

"You selling the rifle?" Billy asks.

"Yep. Thirty caliber. Hardly been fired."

"Got it here?"

Pulls carbine from under bar. Nice. Brass lever. Bluing shines like spilled oil.

"John Wayne cowboy rifle," Bartender says. "Took it in trade on a tab."

"Loaded?"

Yep." Billy checks anyway. Loaded.

"Gonna get me one of them forty-four magnums. You know? One of them Dirty Harry big ass pistols. Smith and Wesson."

Billy aims barrel at bartender.

"Hey, man, be cool. Gun safety and all that shit."

Billy nods.

"Know all about it. First rule of gun safety. Don't hand a loaded weapon to a stranger."

"Don't joke around, man."

"No joke. Empty the register."

"Ya gotta be shittin' me."

"I wouldn't shit you, you're my favorite turd. The money. In a bag please."

Bartender backs up. Eyes fixed on gun barrel. Empties cash register into paper bag."

Other customers go quiet. No one moves. Billy waves barrel at them. "Into the cooler."

They go easy. One takes his beer. One guy, works the punch press, says, "Billy-"

"Shut the fuck up."

Bartender hands Billy bag of money.

"Christ there's only a couple hundred bucks here."

"It's not about the money."

Bartender takes a long look at Billy. Follows others into walk-in cooler in kitchen. Billy closes cooler door. Sticks ice pick into handle. Locked.

The motorcycle is registered. Some other guy's name. Billy rides it out of the state.

# CHAPTER EIGHT

Idaho. Coeur d'Alene. Suburban mall. Close to highway entrance. Parking lot corner. Flathead Twin Theater. "Deliverance" on a double bill with "Scarecrow".

Other screen, "High Plains Drifter". Saturday night. Last show just let in.

Billy sits in parking lot. '72 Corvette. Black on black. Been watching since seven o'clock show. Big night. Box office sold out. Cash registers full. Manager emptied four times. Now adding up receipts, counting cash with cashier. On candy counter.

Dumb move. Has an office. But let's too many kids go early. Saving a dime. Putting cash into bank bag.

Billy eats Ritz crackers from box. Dips them into peanut butter jar. Peter Pan crunchy. Sips Dad's Root beer. Sings along with radio. The Who.

Car pulls up to theater. '70 AMX. Glass packs gurgling. Parks with screech of tires.

Teen boy and girl run into theater, hand in hand. Billy feels a pang. Never had that.

Cashier sells teen couple two tickets. They'll make it in time. Sixteen minutes of trailers before Clint.

Billy lids peanut butter. Closes Ritz box. Steps out of car. Opens trunk. Tiny trunk. Big enough for gym bag. Closes trunk. Walks to AMX. Never drove one before.

Door locked. Sets down gym bag. Unzips. Takes out hammer. T-shirt wrapped around hammer head. Secured with electrical tape.

Billy looks around. No one in sight. Swings hammer. Window shatters. Clears glass. Opens door from inside. Tosses gym bag onto passenger seat. Brushes glass off driver's seat with hammer.

Reaches under dash. Yanks down ignition wire. Takes spare ignition out of gym bag. Puts away hammer. Alligator clips on spare ignition. Hooks up to wires. Engine starts. Good.

Goes back for peanut butter. Box of Ritz. Leaves Root beer. Decides to get Dr Pepper from concession stand.

Takes pistol from gym bag.

Walks to theater.

* * *

Boise. Switches AMX for Nova. Uses Nova to rob National Guard Armory. Easy. No guards. Just fat First Sergeant at desk. Duct tapes him to Steelcase chair.

Trades Nova for Buick Electra. 225. All power. Rides like a toboggan over big drifts.

Parks in an alley. Small town. Outside Billings. Steps out of car. Door shuts with loud thunk. Solid. Heard Detroit engineers design door sounds. Trunk. Hood. Get just the right thunk. Muffler just right. Masculine rumble for muscle cars. Low purr for rich folks. 225 purrs.

Billy finds electrical meter. On alley wall. Next to telephone box. Attaches white phosphorous grenade to circuit into building. Pulls pin. Jumps back. Spoon pops. Grenade flares. Brilliant white. Two thousand degrees. Melts case hardened steel.

Grabs shopping bag from Buick. Trots around corner.

Enters bank.

Dark inside. People mill about. Trying light switches. Man at desk punches adding machine. Useless.

Billy pulls CAR-15 from shopping bag. Loves this gun. Saw it in Armory, grinned. Memories.

Aims CAR at ceiling. Fires burst. Gets their attention.

Everybody freezes. Acoustic tile rains litter. Flutters down slow, like snow.

"Stay cool." Billy speaks soft. "Everyone on the floor except the tellers."

They go down. Billy steps over people. Pauses over guard. Takes the man's pistol. Tosses it into shopping bag.

Holds bag out to first teller. Chubby girl, slides banded money across counter.

"Take it out of the bands." She does. Hands tremble. Billy rifles the greenbacks. Finds dye packet. Tosses it. Shovels cash into bag. Second teller, old woman, Aunt Bee type, the same routine. Third is lying on the floor.

"Lila!" Teller number two hollers. "Get up and give him the goddamned money! Weren't you paying attention?"

Lila rises warily. Empties cash drawer. Billy alert. All five senses cranked. Even a sixth working. Glancing at front door. At folks on the floor. There's always one.

Movement catches his eye. Man at cubicle. Reaches up into desk drawer. Slow and stealthy. There's always one.

"Mister. Don't."

Man looks at Billy. At CAR-15. Billy lowers barrel. Man pulls gun. Revolver. Aims at Billy.

Billy stitches line of bullets across man. Bullets roll him across floor.

A teller screams. Lila.

Billy rushes out. Drives away. Tries to feel bad. Doesn't. Can't.

There's always one.

Billy's new identities. Dead kid names from cemeteries.

Birth certificates from County courthouse. Tells them he lost his in house-fire. Driver's license, presto, New Billy. Always Billy. William. Will. Likes cruising cemetery for names. Wonders about those poor Billys. What would have become of them?

* * *

Wichita. Savings and Loan. Just a mobile home. Trailer on a square of concrete. Dying grass lawn. With a parking lot. Cut power with bolt cutters. Electrical tape on handles. Cut cable writhes across pavement like injured snake. Electricity arcs. Cable snaps like whip. Melts 'Exit' sign.

Billy walks out front door. Casual. CAR in shopping bag. Hops into Camaro. Out of parking lot. Half block to highway.

Heads south.

* * *

Driving. Van. Econoline. Owns this one. Bought in Oklahoma. Steals cars for bank jobs. Returns to van.

Pouring rain. Headlights shine on falling wet, silver daggers. Windshield wipers fight losing battle. Should pull over. Doesn't. Four track tape. The Eagles. "James Dean". Billy sings along.

Tosses empty bank bag out window. Last bank. For a long time. Plenty of money. Stashed at state borders. Doesn't live big. Cheap motels. Fast food joints. Used books.

Passes figure on shoulder. Dark silhouette. Beaten by rain. Sad, woe begotten posture. Billy slows. Stops. Backs up. Checks pistol in door pocket.

Taillights bathe hitchhiker. Woman. Soaked. Illuminated she glistens like glass. Climbs into van.

"Thanks." She shivers. Hugs herself.

Billy eases back onto highway. Signals. Stays under speed limit. Careful about traffic laws.

Turns heat up. Eyes girl.

American Indian. What do they call themselves now? Native American. Not pretty. Handsome. Strong face. Short. Muscular body. No fat. High breasts under wet shirt. No jacket. Long, black hair. Plastered against face, chest.

She looks him over.

"I'll suck you off for twenty bucks."

"I'll give you thirty not to."

She frowns at him.

"Is that an insult or some lame joke?"

"You pick."

Frown fades. She smiles. Crooked grin. Great smile.

"There's some dry clothes in the back."

She thinks a moment. Cautious. Should be. Crawls into the back.

"In that green basket."

His laundry. Just done. Folded neatly. Next to yellow basket. For dirty clothes. Billy is organized.

"Thanks. I'm freezin' my tits off. Cold enough to piss an icicle. Been standin' there a fuckin' hour."

She peels off wet shirt. Tanned. But tits pale. Glow in the dark. She sees him watching. Doesn't cover up.

"Hard to see anyone in this rain," he says. "You could get hit."

She pries off black jeans. No underwear. More tan. More glowing parts.

"Yeah. My own fuckin' fault. Little prick I was ridin' with, an auditor he says, travellin' executioner for bookkeepers, this little peckerhead thinks it's two-for-one day and wants me to blow him again. Woulda told him to bite my ass but he woulda got off on it."

She talks fast. Speed freak? Too much caffeine?

"I'm a business woman, ya know. But shit...every fuckin' john thinks you gotta fall in love with him. You wanna ride the merry-go-round again, you gotta pop for another quarter. Right?"

Tugs on Billy's jeans. A dry t-shirt. Flannel over that. Towels hair dry.

"Then he calls me a fuckin' Spic. A Spic! Told the little jerk off, let me out or I'd cry rape out the window at the first Dudley-Do-Right I saw."

"You got something against Spics?" Billy thinks of the Saenz family. First time in a long time.

"Nope. Don't even like the word. Shouldn't say it, I guess. I'm not gonna. There. But I'm a fuckin' Indian. Native American motherfucker. You gonna call me names, leastways get it right."

"A Native American whore. Right?"

She laughs. Great laugh. From deep inside.

"Yeah. But only temporary. Working my way to California. My brothers are in jail there. Raising bail money on my way."

"How you doin' on that?"

She climbs back up front. Sticks her hands in front of hot air vents.

"They got arrested. Some protest or some shit. Delano, my older brother, he's always agitatin' 'bout some shit or the other."

She drops her head. Ruffles her hair in hot air blast.

"Back home he was always in and outta jail. Fightin', assault they call that, stealin'. B and E. In the pen he got politicized. Became a fuckin' radical. Been organizin' in Cal. I thought he'd kinda gone straight. And he did. Opened an Indian center. Gets our people to march and shit. Still gets his ass busted. Figure that."

Combs her hair with her fingers.

"Blue, my other brother, sweet guy, he'll do anything Delano tells him. And that's his problem. Doesn't have the cojones to take the heat, ya know? Jails suckin' his soul dry. You got anything to eat?"

Cooler behind his seat. Can of deviled ham. Tosses her one. Box of Ritz crackers. Coke in the arm console.

She eats with enthusiasm. Makes little sandwiches. Popped whole into her mouth. Gulps of Coke. Billy's a sipper. A muncher.

"We'll stop for burgers in a bit. I'll buy."

"Hot damn. I found my prince." Cracker crumbs on her shirt. "What's it gonna cost me?"

"What's a square meal worth?"

"Hell, I'd fuck a Republican for a Big Mac." She laughs. With her whole body. "For a large fries I'd even kiss him."

Billy laughs. Loud and hard. First laugh in a long time.

"I'll take an IOU"

She examines him. Doing the math.

"Either you're queer or I've gotten ugly. Uglier. You got some VD phobia? Hell, I'm clean. Fuck, I'm so clean you could eat off me. Or something like that."

That laugh again. Billy joins her.

"I'm Catalina." She smiles. Shy now. Girl changes like the wind. Next she gets serious. "Why not?"

"I'm in a hurry. Need to get some place fast."

"Where?"

"Some place that's not here."

"You on the run?"

She nods. Answers her own question. "You're some kind of outlaw. I know your kind," she says. And she does. "I've seen those eyes before."

Billy drives through the night. Stops to piss. Fuel up. Grab food. Catalina talks, eats, talks. Crawls into the back. Curls into poncho liner. Sleeps.

Sunrise. Welcome to Flagstaff.

Billy cruises into town. Wanders a bit. Finds bus station. Stops.

Non-motion wakes Catalina. "We there?"

"I don't know where 'there' is but this is where we part."

"Oh, right." Disappointment? "Flagstaff."

Billy nods. She ties her shoes. Gathers her clothes. Starts to unbutton shirt. "Keep it."

"Thanks."

She climbs over seat. Wide awake. Opens passenger door. Turns to look at him. He hands her money. A few hundred.

"Why don't you catch a bus the rest of the way."

"Wish I could say no thanks, that you done enough already, but…shit." She takes the bills.

"It's okay," he says. "I just came into a bit of money."

He grins. She grins. Wolf like. Walks around van. Leans into driver's window. "You ever get to LA, look me up. I owe you one. We'll fuck our brains out."

She pops inside. Kisses him. Shy like. Then runs across the street. Stops outside bus station. Waves. Billy waves.

Drives away. Watches in mirror. She enters station. Gone.

* * *

College campus. University. What's the difference? U of Texas. Austin. Huge campus. Billy waits. On a bench. Observing. Strange world. Lots of young faces. Fresh faces. Anybody that innocent? Billy wouldn't know.

Kids. Just kids. Intense discussions. Arguments. 'Cardinal Newman.' 'Perverted priorities.' 'The man.' Three Stooges impressions. Reading while walking. Joking. Necking. Billy feels something. Envy? Grief?

Girl comes over. Sits. Pretty. Cheerleader type. Wind-blown hair. Freckles. Cute. Peasant dress. Tits unfettered. Smells of patchouli. Digs into purse. Canteen of water. Two bananas.

"You don't mind if I have lunch, do you?" So polite. "Would you like a banana?"

"No." He remembers. Courtesy. "Thanks anyway."

"Well, here's what I found so far. In Ohio."

Digs in purse. Notebook. Opens it. Purse must weight fifty pounds.

"Logan, Ohio. 1952. Mister and Mrs. R. Walters. Killed by her ex-husband. Jealousy the apparent motive. Shot both multiple times. Waited for police on the porch. Both children shot. One recovered. Poor girl."

"No," Billy says.

"Chillicothe. '53. Nice sounding place isn't it. Very alliterative. Mrs. Agnes Goodyear. Killed. Her six-year-old son disappeared with the father. She was beaten with a hammer. Allusions as to her moral character."

"No. Go on."

"Rubyville. '53 again. Parents killed by oldest son. Seventeen. Cops said drugs. Of course."

"Next."

"Bowling Green. '54"

Billy's heart leaps. Bowling Green. Maybe this is why he likes the name. The song.

"Mister and Mrs. Dugamon. Bludgeoned to death. Child disappeared."

"How old?" Billy feels a hunger. "The kid. How old?"

"Seven. A daughter. Jennifer. Her body was found four months later when some dog dug it up. That's it."

Billy lets out his breath. Didn't know he was holding it in.

"I'm finishing up Michigan. Lots of murders there. The library has the *Detroit Free Press, Grand Rapids Press,* an Ann Arbor and a Saginaw paper."

"Don't bother."

"What? You're not giving up Mister Williams. We're only half done. Michigan. Wisconsin. I was thinking Pennsylvania. Indiana. Illinois.'

"You'll get paid for the whole job. Don't worry."

"It's not that. Though it helps. I mean, it's not like pouring over microfilm and cataloging these horrible stories is doing my karma any good but…"

"Karma…"

"Maybe if you gave me more data. Narrowed down the parameters."

"There was a cat…" Billy musing. Soft smile. "I've given you what I have."

"I know. A place with snow in the winter. Blueberries. Rural. Parents killed. Child disappeared. '50 to '55. You've piqued my interest Mister Williams."

"I what?"

"Never mind."

"I appreciate your help. But I've decided I don't need this information after all. I mean. What's the point?"

"Well…only you would know."

Billy hands her the envelope. Prepared for this. Thought about it. A lot.

"Here's the rest of your money. And a bonus. Thanks."

Billy rises. Walks away. She watches. He turns back. Looks at her. She wants to follow. He knows. 'Piqued.' That's how you say that.

* * *

New Orleans. Billy loves New Orleans. Even likes the damp decay. Lots of outlaws. Who welcome strangers. Great music. Criminal entrepreneurs embraced. Robs. Steals cars. Great food. Fences everywhere. Cars driven to port. Shipped out. Great bookstores.

Billy in mustache. Long sideburns. His old self pictured in Post Offices everywhere. Jeans. Jean jacket. Cowboy boots from Austin.

Movie theater in Metairie. Heat wave hangout. "Jaws", "Aloha, Bobby and Rose", "The Yakuza", "Mandingo". Hundred and ten outside. Hot wet towel humidity.

Ticket seller. Different girl.

"Where's Cookie?" he asks.

"Didn't show up. Mister Pior's really ticked off."

"Give me a ticket."

"Which show?"

"You pick."

Ticket girl confused. Pushes button. Machine spits "Mandingo".

Billy sees all four movies. Last movie done. Lights up. Auditorium filthy. Candy, popcorn, soda chaos.

Place closing down. Fat woman counting receipts.

Billy pissed off. Cookie a no-show. Nice smile. Cute. Made his day.

Hand in pocket. Thirty-eight Special. Fingers wrap grip. Familiar. Comfortable.

Ticket girl cleaning concession stand. Looks up.

"She didn't come in." Billy's been asking. Between shows. "I called her place. She wasn't there. Sorry."

"No problem."

"No offense but Cookie's kind of a flake," Manager says. Never looks up. Keeps counting.

Billy curls finger around trigger. Clamps jaw. Was going to ask Cookie out. Jet black hair, brilliant smile. Big almond eyes.

Billy gets ready. Slides gun out easy. Careful. Hammer catches on pocket. Smiles at Ticket girl. Thin smile. Jaw clenched.

"If you see her, tell her Billy stopped by. "

Billy idles toward fat woman.

"Tell her I'm leaving town. Just wanted to say goodbye."

Billy stands in front of woman. Gun hidden behind leg.

"That's too bad." Ticket girl leans over counter. Name tag. 'Kathleen.' "I mean, some people wouldn't mind saying goodbye to you. That didn't come out right. You know what I mean?"

A teasing smile. Redhead. Real. A riot of freckles.

Billy nods. Eases gun into back pocket.

"Thanks." Billy leaves. No big thing. Doesn't need the money.

Parking lot. Customized pick up. Next to Billy's Corvette. Ford 150. Big ass tires. Custom paint. Lots of lights. On top of cab. On grill. Chrome wheels. Sparkling clean. Drugstore cowboy truck.

Three teenage boys. Letter jackets. Giggling like girls. Knuckle hung bottles of beers. Cool.

One hunched over Billy's ride. Prying 'Corvette' logo off. Swiss Army knife.

"What the fuck you doing?"

Kid turns. Squints at Billy. Drunk eyes.

"Nothin'." Snotty.

"Get your ass outa here." Billy tired. Doesn't want this. Kid shakes his head. Smiles. Challenging. Looks to buddies. Got my back look. They do.

"He's almos' done." More giggles.

Knife blade inserted. Between car body, logo. Billy clenches. Fist. Jaw. Logo pops. One end. Hangs.

Billy sighs. Pulls gun.

"Leave now." Voice soft. "Or I kill you on the spot."

Calm. Kids startled. Scared. For a second. Then booze takes over. Or the stupid.

"Fuck you." Kid with the knife. "You ain't gonna kill nobody over a dumb thing like this. "

He nods to himself. The logic is clear. He thinks of something else. "Maybe I'll take that gun away from you."

Takes a step toward Billy. "Dwayne, don't." One has sense.

Another step. Billy shoots. Bullet spins the boy. Pretty pirouette. Legs can't keep up. Falls.

Other two freeze.

"Why'd you go and do that?"

Billy aims at questioner. Boy closes his eyes. Tears form. Other boy runs. "Consequences," Billy says. Shot boy whines. Cat sounds.

Billy lowers gun. Stuffs back in pocket. Barrel hot. Steps into 'Vette. Drives away. Van parked in Metairie.

# CHAPTER NINE

Los Angeles. Hollywood, of all places. A bar. Off Hollywood Boulevard. Boardner's. A dive. With character. Career winos. One Social Security check from living like a coyote. Forty years of bad booze reek. Sad stories. Rat pack photos behind bar. Sinatra, Sammy, Martin. Eddie Fisher? Some signed. Used to be the place. Sadder. Jolson on the jukebox, for Chrissake.

Billy orders a Coke. With a cherry. And some juice. Heads for the back. Night. Lushes and barflies come out with the moon. Out of towners. Prowlin' for poon. White plastic shoes. Matching belt. Pitiful. Ozzie Nelson types cruisin' the gutter.

Billy takes a table. Back against the wall. Nurses the Coke. Tips bartender a twenty. Lets him linger.

Watches open front door. Parade of pervs, tourists. Guitar slinging rockstar wannabees. Runaways. Sad sacks and lonely hearts. Crazies. Slick dudes and pop tarts. Immigrants and has-beens.

Eventually, Catalina walks in. Red dress. Slit up to her ass. Bad wig. High heels. Feet hurting. Looks ridiculous. Sits at the bar. Trawling for a short time sugar daddy.

Billy watches.

She doesn't see him. Dark corners at Boardner's. For a reason.

Gray haired geezer enters. Past his prime. Leisure suit. Short. Roly poly. Thin hair oiled to scalp. Moves to her. Leans into wig.

"I know you." He leers.

Catalina squints. Bartender knows her. Beer and shot without an order. Catalina nurses beer. Ignores geezer. He persists.

"Night before last. Holiday Inn. Me and you. See, I do know you."

"You mean you fucked me. You don't know me."

Geezer gawks. Taken aback.

"Oh, yeah. We kinda made love."

"Kinda?" Catalina's tired. So tired. "Mister, I'm off duty. Buzz off, will ya?"

"Okay. But…don't you remember me?"

"Sure. I remember you. You were the best. I came so hard I lost my short-term memory. In other words you fucked my brains out. Ruined me for any other man.

Drove me right out of the business. Now leave me the fuck alone. I've had a long night."

"I was hoping we could get together. Again. You know?"

"And 'make love'? Wish in one hand, shit in the other. See which one fills first."

"He, cut me some slack here, toots. I'm just trying to throw some business your way."

"And I'm telling you I'm not in business right now. Even God got a day off for Chrissake."

The geezer makes a grab. Catalina yanks her arm away. Billy rises. Walks over. Takes geezer's wrist. Twists. "Hey! Oww!"

"Go away." Billy suggests.

Catalina surprised. Grins. Takes Billy's arm.

"Yeah, 'toots.' You wouldn't want to piss off my fiancé, would you?" They leave.

Geezer gawps.

* * *

Billy drives. Molester van, Catalina calls it. Over the hills. Santa Monica mountains, she says. Billy's seen mountains. These aren't.

The valley. Smoggy sprawl.

Tiny house. Poor neighborhood. Volvo on blocks. Paint job sun matted. Dead grass. Scruffy palms. Scraggly lemon tree. Graffiti scars on every wall.

Hot wind. Desert dry.

Man on the porch. Sprawled. Plastic chair. Sullen. Pitted face. Black hair past shoulders. Whittling. No - carving. Broom handle. Wasted straws broom still attached. Elegant scrimshaw.

"Delano, this here's Billy." Catalina does the intro. Delano looks up. Angry eyes.

"Just 'cause you bring 'em home don't mean I got to meet 'em."

"He's the one helped us on the bail money when you...aw, fuck it."

She takes Billy inside. Screen door slams behind them. Furniture mismatched and worn. Thrift store styling.

Young man slouched on sofa. Same long hair. Aviator shades. Watching TV. Bottle of cheap wine.

"Blue, Billy. Billy, Blue."

Billy nods. Blue nods.

"My baby brother." Catalina smiles.

Blue eyes Billy over shades. Eyes glassy. Turns to Catalina.

"You working?" Blue asks.

"No! This here's a friend. He did me...us, a favor. I promised to fuck his brains out."

Blue laughs. Billy uncomfortable. Tries a laugh. Fails. Reaches into pocket. Thrusts twenty to Blue.

"Maybe you'd like to get us something to eat."

Blue looks at the money. Looks at Billy. Seems hurt. Billy more uncomfortable. Fucked up. How to fix?

"No call for that, Billy." Catalina smooths salve on the wound.

"No offense meant. I just…felt like a party. I buy – you fly?"

"Party? In that case twenty don't cut it." Catalina brightens. "Twenty bucks don't even buy a decent toot."

She digs into her bra. Tosses more twenties Blue's way. Blue grins. Billy throws in a couple more bills. Blue grins. Gathers money.

"Anything you want in particular?" Blue asks Billy.

"Some Dr Pepper," Billy says.

"Chicken. White meat. Extra crispy." Catalina instructs.

Blue goes.

Billy and Catalina fuck. Not making love. Fuck. Hard, physical work. Sweaty, work. Making each other come. Repeatedly. Bodies shine. Slick.

Tiny bedroom. Mattress wall to wall. Red t-shirt over lamp. Red glow makes room hotter.

Radio plays. Santana. "Sighing Wind, Crying Beasts."

Billy fucks her. From behind. Pounds her. Her head beats wall. Sticky bodies slap noisily.

Catalina on top. Breath hisses between clenched teeth. Head back, hair waterfalls. Reaches cleft of her ass. Billy cups breasts. Holding. An offering. She comes. Screams.

They are one. Some animal. Head to balls. Mouth to cunt. Wrapped in flesh. Clinging. Clawing. Rolling across bed. On to floor.

Rest. Sore knees. Sore cock. Scratched back. Stinging with sweat salt. A good hurt. Catalina's face raw. Beard burn.

Shower. Soap each other. Laughing. She lathers his pubes. He does hers.

"Careful." He flinches. "It's a little tender."

"You should bitch." Catalina rubs harder. "I'm gonna walk bow legged for a week."

She squeezes Prell. Half the tube. Suds up his hair. Sculpts it. Alfalfa spike. Wings. Horns. Giggles. Adds a foam mustache, goatee.

"Where you staying?" she asks.

"I'm not."

She reacts. Not happy.

"I got some work to do. Then I'm gone."

"You could stay a day or two. For you, I'd take a vacation. We could both do the vacation thing."

"Vacation?" Billy muses. Never had one.

"Bet I could convince you." She teases. Hands slide down. Caress his groin. Massages his cock. A good hurt. He responds.

"Bet I could talk you out of it." Billy grins. Slides his hand. Cups bristly crotch. Inserts tip of finger. Catalina gasps.

They stare down. Eye to eye. Hands moving. Probing.

"We could be nice together." She whispers. Purrs. "Just a little while. You and me. On the bed."

"What do you call what we just did?"

"That was good fucking. This would be…nice."

"Nice."

"Nice." She draws the word out.

Billy jerks. Muscle spasm. She hit a tender spot. An erogenous spot.

That's not all. Billy feels something. A longing. For what? It scares him. But he can't stop.

"We'll be nice now." She rasps. And gasps. Billy's building her passion.

"Gentle now." She moans. "Gentle me."

They kiss. Soft this time. Doing the gentle thing. Water cascades over them. Skims away the lather.

Back to the bed. Make love to Al Green. Van Morrison.

Catalina places small kisses. His neck. Face. Eyelids. Her tongue wets his lips. His nipples. Gentle worship.

Billy has to hold back. Succumb. Difficult at first. Then he sinks under. Willing to drown.

After. Catalina lays back. Billy hovers. Admiring. In the half light. Kisses her ear. Passes hand over her. Back of hand. Fist hair brushes her flesh. Rise of breast. Dark areole. Ridge of hip. Gooseflesh trails behind. She trembles.

*  *  *

Dressed. Cloth abrasive over raw skin. Enter living room. Delano on sofa. Reading paper. Glares at Billy.

"What's the hap' bro'?" Catalina asks.

"The Feds just gave a chunk of our land to the timber and mining companies."

"It's not theirs to give, is it?"

"Tell them that. Department of Interior works for the white man. Not us." Delano's eyes stab Billy.

"The rich white man," Billy says.

"Where's Blue?" Catalina asks. Her hand never leaves Billy. Lingers on his shoulder. Hip. Nests inside his fingers. "He went to fetch everybody some chicken."

"You gave him money?" Delano off the couch.

"Yeah." Catalina defensive. "He's okay now. Really. He looks a lot better. Just sips a little wine to keep him copacetic. Round the corners off."

"You gave him money." Delano shakes his head. "With Checci's people looking for his ass. You know if Blue's got enough for some shit he's gonna try to score."

Delano swerves from anger to despair.

Billy heads for the door. Catalina's hand slips away. He feels the absence.

"Gotta go," he says.

Delano ignores him. Glares at Catalina.

"How much did you give him?"

"Forty. Sixty bucks." Catalina crestfallen. "For a toot."

She turns to Billy. At the door.

"Hey…maybe again, huh?"

Sad eyes. Little girl eyes. Billy feels the pull. Fights it.

"Yeah, I'd like that."

Steps out. Van keys in hand.

Sitting on the street. Blue. Back against van. Face bloody. Bruised. Eye swollen shut. Worked over. Clothes torn. Dirty. Knee scrapped. Oozing.

Blue clutches crushed Colonel bucket to chest. Quart of Dr Pepper cradled in arm.

Looks up at Billy. Smiles. Lips cracked, bleeding. Broken tooth. Smiles like little kid.

"I lost your change, dude."

Billy helps boy up. Fried chicken rains onto pavement. Blue bends. Picks up a leg. Careful precise movements. Kid is hurting. Puts leg back in bucket.

Billy helps him to house. Catalina sees them coming. Through the screen door. Steps out. Delano behind her. Brother comes to help.

"Blue." Catalina moans. "I'm sorry."

Billy lets her take Blue.

"'S'okay," Blue says. "I almos' had a good time." Tries to laugh.

Delano turns to Billy. "Get. Go. Now."

Billy turns.

"Wait. Wait," Blue says.

Hands Billy Dr Pepper. Billy smiles. Takes it. Catalina has tears. For Blue? For Billy? Billy wants to do something. For her. At a loss. Walks away.

At car. Looks back. Catalina in doorway. Eyes meet. He turns away. Into van. Drives.

* * *

Los Angeles. Bank robbers wet dream. Park on the freeway. Raise the hood. Car trouble. Stolen Buick. Kit bag in front seat. Tools of the trade. Walk down embankment. Through the brush.

Chain link fence. Bolt cutters from bag. Cut hole. Cutters back in bag.

Other side of the fence. Back of Vons. Big chain grocery/drugstore. Short row of small shops. Surround huge parking lot. In center. Washington Mutual Bank.

Billy walks across lot. Reaches into bag. Wraps fist around grip. CAR-15.

A minute inside. No more than three. Just the cashiers. Put the scare in them. Fill the bag. No bills in wrappers. Has teller unwrap. Fan bills. Dye packet falls out.

Fill the bag.

And out. Cool walk across lot. Wary. But cool. No attention paid. Two boys skateboard. Zoom past.

Walk back behind Vons. Back through fence. Hears alarm behind him. Strident bell. Ringing. Ringing.

Billy drives away. Merges with traffic. One of eight million cars.

* * *

Three banks. In three weeks. Bank number four. Bank of America. Culver City. Ease in. Ease out. Walk up embankment. Cop motorcycle behind his car. Stolen Monte Carlo. Highway patrol. Tight pants. Knee boots. Mirrored aviators. Helmet. Hollywood style cop. Peering into car window.

Sees Billy. Billy smiles.

Cop starts to smile back. Then stops. Frowns. Hears alarm down hill. Does the arithmetic. Aha. Hand to holster. Billy already has hand in bag.

Fires. Through bag. Bullet erupts from fabric. Short burst. Three rounds. Just like Army taught him. Cop takes all three in chest. Knocked back. Rolls down embankment.

Billy steps over to edge. Looks down. Mistake. BAM! Muzzle blast flares. Cop has fired.

Billy falls to knees. Leg doesn't work. Pulls himself up. Hops to car. Slams down hood. Drags self to driver's side. Throws bag across seat. Crawls inside. Drives off.

Parks Monte Carlo at Fox Hills Mall. Employee parking. Close to van. Braces self. In pain. Pool of blood on floor matt. Ties tourniquet with belt. Tightens.

Sets jaw. Steps out. Check for observers. Grabs bag. Limps to van. Leaves bloody footprints. Drives away. Slow.

Night. Catalina's house. Parked across street. Yellow light inside. Front door open. TV light flickers across screen door.

Tries to move. Gasps in pain. Clenches teeth. Closes eyes. Lays back head. Can't move.

Honks horn. Once. Twice. Three times.

Catalina at screen door. Silhouetted. Steps onto porch. Recognizes Billy's van. Heads straight for him. Big smile.

"Boy, you are full of surprises."

Leans into window. Frowns. Billy must look like shit.

"I need a place to stay for a few days."

"Sure. I still owe you one." Concerned.

"I thought we even-upped last time."

"Oh, no. I enjoyed that too much for it to be a payback."

Billy tries to get out again. Doesn't make it. Falls out of van. Catalina bends over him. He looks up at her. Love that face.

"I got a little problem."

Tries to rise.

Blacks out.

* * *

"Momma? Daddy?"

"I gotta pee. Momma?"

Shuffle through house. Everything so big. Cant' reach door knobs. Daddy is asleep. On kitchen floor. Eyes open. Scary.

"Momma?"

Momma asleep. Living room floor. Eyes open. Man on top of her. Knows this man…

"Mama?"

Billy opens his eyes. Dark. On a bed. Catalina. Next to him. Sleeping. On lounge chair. Plastic and aluminum. Billy rubs face. Bristly. He shivers.

Catalina wakes.

"What's wrong, babe?"

"Cold."

Blanket. Trembling increases. Catalina lays next to him. Embraces him. Billy relaxes. Closes eyes.

* * *

Days later. Breakfast in bed. Trix. Catalina watches. Concerned. Measuring.

"Hey." She speaks. Cigarette smoke escapes mouth. "You almost look like a human being. Close enough to pass, I guess."

She chuckles.

Billy thinks. Am I human? Manages a smile. Catalina misinterprets. Laughs with him.

"The boys want to talk to you." She takes his empty bowl. "You up to it?"

He nods. She leaves. He is so tired. To the bone. Straightens up. Back against pillows. Try to look strong.

Catalina returns. Delano, Blue behind. A third man. Squat, solid, ugly.

"You know Delano. Blue." She points to third man. "This here's Joe. He fixed your leg up."

"I was a medic. Once." Joe smiles. "Nam."

Short silence. Delano distracted. Peeling wallpaper from wall. Blue fidgets. Scratching scabs on arms. Catalina holds Billy's gym bag. Billy notices. Tries to distract. Turns to Joe.

"You did a good job."

"Yeah? Thanks. I ripped off some tetracycline for you."

"I owe you." Billy means it.

"That's what we came about." Delano. Head of the family.

"We figure…Cat taking care of you and all that shit. We took five hundred bucks from your bag."

Catalina drops bag on bed. Thunk. Rattle. Silence again. Waiting for Billy's reaction.

"It's fair," he says. And means it.

"We needed the bread to buy some guns," Delano says.

"None of my business." Means it.

Delano nods. Steps toward door. Cue for Blue and Joe. They leave. Catalina puts bag on floor. Within Billy's reach.

"In case you're interested, the cop's gonna make it. Live."

"His luck."

She waits for more. Nothing comes.

"Let's change those sheets. They're getting' kind of crusty."

She helps him rise. The world spins. She holds him. Close. Comforting. Brings back memories. Vague. Just the feeling. Comforting. Safe.

"Give Joe another five hundred," he tells her.

She nods. "How would you like a bath?"

"I'd like that a whole helluva lot."

* * *

Billy recovers. Catalina crochets. Mom taught her. Sold doilies to the tourists.

"Hell of a comedown for an Apache Warrior Woman," Catalina says.

Billy rolls thread into a ball. Listens.

"Warrior woman," he says to prod. Likes to hear her talk.

"You best be careful around me. I'm the direct descendant from Lozen, sister of Victorio. He rode with Geronimo, lead the Chiricahua and Mescalaros against the U.S. Army. The Mexes killed him. Lozen could outride, outshoot, out hunt and out fight any man or woman and did it with grace,"

"Like you."

"I wish. She could find the enemy for Victorio. She'd stick

out her arms and chant. 'Upon the earth, on which we live, Usen has Power, this Power is mine, for locating the enemy, I search for that enemy, which Usen the Great, can show to me."

Drops crocheting. Puts out her arms. Head back. Speaks to ceiling. Billy impressed. Can see the warrior woman.

"Who's Usen?" he asks.

"A God. The life giver. Lozen could feel the enemy's location by tingling in her arms."

She sways, arms outstretched. Swings back and forth. Stops. One arm aimed at Billy. Finger points at him.

"I'm not your enemy," he says.

"Prove it." She comes to him. All mouth and caresses. Billy aches. But succumbs. It hurts. But soon the pain forgotten.

* * *

Weeks later. Billy can walk. Catalina takes him out. Block party. Vacant parking lot. Old chain grocery store closed. Fled the neighborhood. Goodwill store adjacent.

Latino band on a flatbed truck. Latin rock with accordion. Killer accordion player. Billy recognizes some songs. Saenz memories. Mexican food from stalls. Carts. Wagons. La Raza registration table. Games. Penney tosses. Loop tosses. Carnival games. For nickels and dimes. All doing business. Mostly Chicanos. Few blacks. Few whites. Few Asians. Kids eating candy apples. Cotton candy. Banderas. Conchas.

Billy and Catalina sit on a curb. Eat pineapple on a stick. Blue and Delano join them. Sipping cheap wine. Passing paper bagged bottle between them.

Blue points out car. Black Firebird.

"'Nother coupla jobs and I'm gonna get me one of them jobbies. Pontiac was an Indian. A chief," he says.

"He didn't invent the goddamned car." Delano always angry. "They wouldn't even let him work on the fucking production line. The white man stole his name, his fucking legend, his fucking soul to sell their goddamned machine."

"It's still a cherry fucking car." Blue nods to himself. "What kinda car would you get?"

"A Porsche. It's German. The Germans never did anything to our people."

"No," Catalina says. "They had the Jews."

That makes Blue laugh. It's a good laugh. Puts his heart into it.

Catalina pulls Billy away. Tosses pineapple sticks into gutter. Billy limping. Leg still stiff. Sore. He leans on her. Doesn't need to. Likes it.

They watch the band. A corridor. Sad. Catalina nudges him. Points.

Two kids dancing. Slow. Twelve, thirteen. Fingers entwined. Sway to song. In love. Eye to eye.

"God, were we ever that innocent?" Catalina asks.

Song ends. Band segues. "Stay." An oldie. In Spanish.

"I never had an innocent day in my life," Billy says.

Billy chokes up. Ready to cry. Pulls himself back. Catalina embraces him. Starts to slow dance. Billy is reluctant.

"Oh, your leg. Sorry."

"I'm fine." Can't refuse her. His leg pains him. Still he persists.

"The leg's getting better every day. I'll be going soon." He feels her muscles tense. "I'd like you to go with me."

There, he said it. Days and nights of pondering.

She pulls back. Looks him in the eyes.

"You know me," he says.

"You kiddin'?" she smiles. That crooked grin. "Hell, I cleaned up after you when you shit the bed."

Her joke a defense. He knows how she works.

"I've always been alone," he says. Thinks. "More or less. I don't want to be alone anymore. No, that's not true. I can take being alone. But I can't take being without you."

Bigger smile. All teeth and gums. Kisses him. A big one. Pulls back. Frowns.

"What about the boys? I can't leave them alone. Especially now."

"Why now?"

"They're planning something big."

"They can take care of themselves."

"No. They can't. They ain't done this kinda shit before. Delano's an organizer, not a gangster. This is gangster stuff. And Blue...he's a baby. They need me. Otherwise their wheels kinda come off."

The song ends. Silence for a moment. Stop dancing.

"Maybe you could help the," she says.

"I always work alone."

"But you just said-"

"Work is different. I don't have to trust anyone but me. I don't have to worry about anyone."

She steps away. Walks away. He follows. Touches her shoulder. She stops, turns.

"I can't go nowhere 'less I know my brothers are...safe."

He nods.

"You know?"

He nods again.

"They need me."

"I need you."

She hugs him.

"Maybe we can work something out," he says.

She kisses him. Repeatedly. They dance again. Near an old couple. Gray haired man. Zorro mustache. Her black bouffant tickles his chin. Backs stiff. Regal dancing. Old woman full of grace. Billy admires. Old man winks at him. Billy winks back. His first wink.

"Oh, shit." Catalina stiffens.

Two cops standing over Blue, Delano. Boys still on curb.

"Maybe they're looking for me." Billy looks for escape.

"No." Catalina shakes her head. "They arrested some dude in Riverside for your thing. Cop you shot even ID'd him."

Billy and Catalina approach.

"Don't be stupid Tonto." The cop taps Delano on the head with long ass flashlight. Thunk.

"You don't know who you're fucking with. Checci's gonna put you in a world of hurt," the other cop says.

"We know you're the asshole behind all this, Chief. You and your doper brother here. I'm tellin' ya. Stay clear of the man or you're dead meat."

He whacks Delano again. Bigger thunk. Must hurt. Delano glares at the cop. Silent hate. Eyes embers of violence.

Other cop drives knee into Blue's face. Nose cracks. Bleeds. Blue doesn't respond. Leans over. Drains onto pavement.

"Problem here?" Billy asks.

Cops turn on Billy.

"No problem," cop says. "Unless you want one."

"Not anymore," other cop says. "Tonto's finished with the stupid. Right?"

Catalina takes Billy's handkerchief. Makes Blue tilt head back. Wipes his lip.

"We should get you and icy. Put it on your nose."

"Make it a cherry. I like cherry." Blue tries to smile. Hurts.

Billy watches cops. Until they drive away.

They're right," Billy says. "You been stupid."

"I don't have to take this shit from you, too." Delano spits.

"You keep ripping off Checci's runners and bag men, there's bound to be some payback. All he has to do is put some back up with them. One day you hit the wrong one…it's over."

Billy knows. Overheard conversations.

"We ain't backing off. Not after what he did to Blue."

"That's really stupid. Revenge is for suckers." Billy shakes his head. "There's no profit in it."

"You can say that. You got no pride to defend," Delano says.

"Yeah. You don't understand," Blue says. All nasal. "White man."

Says it like a curse. First time Blue pissed at Billy.

"Don't give me any of your Indian bullshit. You're no more Indian than I'm a fucking German, or an Irish man, or a Jew. Give me a break. There haven't been any real Indians for a hundred years."

"Billy!" Catalina outraged.

Billy stops.

"A real Indian would go to war," Billy says.

They stare at him. "Let me help you with this Checci thing."

# CHAPTER TEN

Just like casing a bank. Like recon on a 'ville. Billy watched. For days. Checci had bad habits. Everybody has bad habits. Everybody has a routine. Except Billy. He tells himself.

Checci had habits. Checci had routines. Breakfast at Norm's. Every morning 9:30.

Toasters at every table. Wheat toast for Checci. Sausage patty. Cottage cheese.

Fruit bowl. Ketchup on cottage cheese. Coffee. Two cups. Reads LA Times. After second cup – men's room. 10:05 to 10:20. Morning dump. Takes sports section with.

No office for Checci. Rides limo. Lincoln Towne Car. Making stops all day. Used car lots. Record store. Porn theater. Jerry's Deli for lunch. Meetings at every stop.

Various characters. Always a thug or two in the mix. Carrying. Bulge under windbreaker. In back of pants. Hands slide there when tense. Door slams.

Strangers approach. Thugs beat man in alley. Behind record store. Break a finger in deli parking lot.

Lunch with men just like Checci. Lots of laughs. Some serious business. Thugs eat at separate table. Checci likes tuna melt. Eats pickles from other plates.

After lunch – more stops. More meets. Head shops. Newsstands. Restaurants. Another porn theater. Liquor stores. Paper bags handed over. Tosses in limo trunk. Meets in parking garages. Vacant lots. More paper bags.

Dinner at Cock 'N' Bull. Sunset. More men in suits. Like Checci. No tie for Checci. He likes the French Dip. With fresh horseradish. So does Billy.

Four days watching. Catalina and boys itchy. Billy bullies. Perseveres.

Friday morning. Billy at Norm's counter. Eggs over hard, hash browns. Makes toast. Waitress brings marmalade. Hates marmalade. Asks for alternative. Gets raspberry. Puts it on his eggs.

Checci at booth. Small man. Bald. Gray eyes. Gray suits. Gray pallor. Watered down man.

Three after ten. Checci pulls sports section. Strides to back. Driver clears men's room. Checci enters. Driver watches front door.

Billy leaves Catalina at counter. Didn't eat her omelet.

Billy approaches men's room. Driver stops Billy. Knife thin man. Black chauffer suit. Cap.

"It's busy," Driver says.

"Unless you want me to piss in your shoe, step aside." Billy winces. Need to go look. Pushes past Driver. Into bathroom. Driver follows. Door swings shut behind.

Billy whirls. Gun barrel into Driver's eye socket. Finger to Billy's lips. Shhhh. Takes Driver's gun. Small Beretta. Shoulder holster.

Pushes Driver's shoulder. Sits him on tiled floor. Billy opens door. Blue and Delano waiting. Enter.

Toilet flushes. Checci steps out. Brothers there. Each puts gun to Checci's temple.

Checci flinches. Recovers.

"You're dead," he says.

Blue nervous. Twitchy. Thumbs back hammer. "Wrong. Try again asshole."

"On the floor," Billy orders.

"There's piss on the floor." Checci whines. Delano pushes Checci to sit.

Billy nods to Delano. Delano slips out door. Standing guard.

Billy holds gun. On Checci and Driver. Blue wraps copper wire around Driver's wrists. Around Checci's wrists. Tight.

"You cocksuckers are in deep shit." Checci growls. Deep voice. "You know who I am?"

Billy kicks him. Once. Checci grunts. Blue finishes wiring wrists.

"Up." Billy orders. Checci doesn't move. Billy grabs fistful of hair. Hauls him up. Driver rises. Billy knocks on door.

Outside Delano nods to Catalina. She pulls smoke grenade. Pulls ring. Pops spoon. Drops under table. Walks to front door.

Billowing purple smoke. Spews across floor. Fills restaurant. Patrons react. Shout. Yell. Scream. Dash for door.

Billy and Blue push Checci and Driver. Into melee. Delano rushes ahead.

Out to van. Delano slides side door open. Checci and Driver pushed inside. Catalina into shotgun seat. Billy and Blue in back.

Delano drives away.

* * *

Checci's house. Checci's mansion. In the hills. Big brick wall. Iron gates. Security pad on pole. Delano pulls alongside. Billy gun-taps Checci on head.

"The longer you play along, the longer you live. Everything goes right, I might let you stay that way."

Waits for Checci to absorb.

"The gate code." Taps Checci again.

"Fuck you." Checci smirks. A challenge. Do your worst.

Billy turns to Delano. "One oh six six." Watched Driver do it four times. Three buttons have paint rubbed off. Just watched for order.

Checci is surprised. Billy smiles. Then clubs him with gun. In face. Gashes forehead. Bleeds a lot there.

"That's a warning. Don't fuck around."

Delano reaches through van window. Punches code. Nothing happens. Everyone looks at Billy.

"It takes a second."

Clunk. Clack. The whir of a motor. Gate slowly swings out. Everybody relaxes. Except Billy. He knows. Hard part is coming.

Delano parks next to house. Billy tosses Catalina Checci's keys. Front door is unlocked. Billy prods Checci inside. Blue pushes Driver. Delano and Catalina follow.

Big ass entry way. Stairs going up. Then living room. Big as a basketball court.

On the sofa a man. Pants around his ankles. Before him a woman, kneeling.

Checci spits. "Shit."

Both heads pop up. Stare at group. Blowsy woman, over-weight. Tits hanging out. She stuffs them back. Like putting socks in a drawer. Man yanks up pants. Shoves shirt in.

"For fuck"s sake. Unk?" Checci shakes his head. Disgusted. Annoyed. "Lainie?" Blue laughs.

Unk and Lainie see the guns. The bound hands. "Oh, shit," Unk says.

"Frisk him," Billy tells Blue.

Blue walks over, runs hands over old man.

"Not like he's carrying anything but four semi-hard-on inch-es." Blue laughs again.

"Anyone else in the house Lainie?" Billy asks.

"No. Just us." Smeared lipstick on her face.

"Catalina, watch the front door." Billy orders. She takes CAR-15.

"Delano search the place. See if she's right." Delano nods to Billy, takes shotgun and disappears. Billy hears doors open, shut.

Billy pushes Checci to sofa. "Everybody sit."

Lainie sits. Unk sits. Checci stays upright. Billy pushes him in chest. Checci falls into sofa. Blue puts Driver in chair.

"Now let's make this easy on you folks," Billy says. "Because the hard way's gonna hurt."

"The safe's behind the TV." Lainie spits out. "Nobody's got the combination but him."

Checci glares at her. "Cunt."

Blue goes to the huge Advent TV. Rolls it away from wall. Panel behind. Blue slides it open. A safe. Big as a fridge.

"Open it," Billy tells Checci.

"Fuck you." Checci shakes his head. "I do, I'm dead."

Billy nods. Shoots Driver.

Everyone jumps. Delano rushes down the stairs, stares. Catalina appears.

"Billy." Catalina gasps.

He looks at her. She is astonished. What did she expect? Blue and Delano stare at body. Hole in Driver's forehead. Eyes bulging. Arms, legs twitch. Then still.

Lainey folds. Head on knees. Sobbing.

Gunfire. Three shots. Catalina. CAR-15 barrel smokes.

Unk jumps, falls. Looks up. Angry. Blood bubbles from his chest. Pistol in hand. Tiny gun. Pant leg slid up. Ankle holster.

Billy glares at Blue.

"I, I…didn't see it." Blue looks away.

Billy nods to Catalina. She puffs up with pride. Unk dies. Eyes go up, slide to look at floor.

Back to Checci. Flicks of fear in his eyes. But he beats it back. "I was going to fire him anyway."

Voice raspy but steady. Licks his lips. Keeps eyes on Billy's gun. Billy puts barrel to Lainey's head. She squeals. Cries louder.

"Billy no."

Delano lays hand on Billy's elbow. Billy looks at him. Vicious look. Hard. "Don't fuck around in my business."

"Go ahead. I like her less'n I like him." Checci glances at Unk. Smiles. Wolf grin.

"Tourniquet him." Billy orders.

Delano takes wire from pocket. Winds it around Checci's thigh. "Tight. Or he bleeds out before we get what we want." Billy instructs.

Catalina goes back to the door. Glances over her shoulder. Nervous. Doesn't like this part of plan.

"You're cutting off my circulation." Checci complains. Scared now.

"Exactly," Billy says.

Shoots. Foot explodes. White bone. Red meat. Blood and gristle.

Checci screams. Rolls to floor. Breath hisses between teeth.

"We can work our way up that leg," Billy tells him. "The knee is the worst. Then we got a whole 'nother leg. And if we need them, two arms. Hands, elbows and all."

"You dumb cocksuckers will pay for this." Checci reaches for foot. Changes mind. Reaches again. Pulls back. Bound hands, fingers wiggling like spider legs.

Blue stands over Checci. Kicks wounded leg.

"Payback's a motherfucker, ain't it." Blue grins.

"Take him to the safe," Billy tells him. Delano nudges Blue. Both drag Checci to safe.

Checci whines in pain. They hold him up next to safe. Checci dials. Misses. Dials again. Tries handle. Won't open.

"Take a breath, try again. Slow this time," Billy says.

Checci dials again. Tries handle. It turns.

"Don't open it. We'll do that," Billy says. Turns to Delano. "Hideaway gun."

Delano nods, lets Checci fall. Steps to safe. Opens. Tosses thirty-eight Special. Nods to Billy. Then looks into safe.

"Oh, mother." Delano whispers. Blue giggles. Catalina comes over to look.

Delano and Blue pull boxes out. Shoe boxes. Full of greenbacks. Ten shoe boxes. Catalina laughs out loud.

"Oh man. Fuck me." Blue reverent. Discovers shrink wrapped package. "Look what we got. There's snow in California."

"Coke?" Delano asks.

"It ain't baby powder."

"Leave it." Billy orders.

"No way, Jose." Blue astounded at the idea. Tosses drugs into money bag. What to do? Shoot Blue? Billy looks to Catalina. She shrugs. Billy unhappy.

"That's it," Delano says. Safe empty.

Billy turns to Checci. Aims.

"NO!" Catalina moves fast. Knocks Billy's gun hand. Bullet pocks wall. Everyone freezes. Catalina angry. "You made a deal with him," she accuses.

"I lied," he admits. He looks at Checci, Lainey. Checci fading. Lainey the same. Given up. Billy considers.

"Okay. Knock 'em out."

Catalina walks over. Hesitates above Checci.

"Do it." Billy orders. "Or I kill 'em. Both of them."

She swings machine gun. Clocks Checci in head. He goes down. Still conscious. Catalina has to hit him again. And again. And again.

Delano clubs Lainey. Back of the head. Very efficient. One solid blow. She's out.

Everyone heads for the door. Blue laughs. Sounds like his sister.

* * *

Another hot day. Catalina in panties and t-shirt. Panties from Frederick's of Hollywood. Shopping spree after Checci.

Billy in jeans only. Lounge on sofa. After sex. She licks his nipple.

"Salty." She grins.

"Where are they?"

"They'll be back." She picks up crochet needle. Metallic green. Crocheting a spirit catcher for Billy. Fingers dance. Thread chain grows. Billy likes to watch.

"Been a long time."

"They'll be back," she insists. "They sell the drugs, and we all go to the Res. You'll like New Mexico. Weather is fiiine. You got money you can live gooood."

"They're not back by sunset...I'm gone," he tells her, meaning it. Does like the drug bit. Doesn't like it at all. Out of his control. Out of his expertise.

"Don't sweat it." She rises. "Want something to drink?" Heads to kitchen.

"Ice water."

"We should do this thing again. There's lots of rich bad guys out there. And what can they do? Go to the cops?"

"Never again." Billy is adamant. "Blue was high."

"But he got it done." Fridge door opened. Rattle of ice cubes. "He needs a little something to smooth out the bumps. He actually does better with..."

The front door explodes. Flies in. Lands on floor. Crash.

"POLICE!!" Cops bust in. Helmets and body armor. Machine guns and shotguns.

Billy looks to Catalina. She in kitchen doorway. Two glasses in hand.

Cop trips in doorway. Another cop falls over him. Shotgun booms.

Catalina does backward flip. Skids across floor.

Crash. Back door. Shouts. Billy deaf.

Billy crawls to Catalina. Cop kicks Billy. He sprawls. Cop cuffs Catalina. Her arms limp. Click click.

"Catalina." Billy calls to her. No answer.

Billy cuffed. Behind back. Rights read. Cops take off helmets. Billy stares at cop with shotgun. Red hair. Looking guilty. Hispanic cop comes over, pats Red on shoulder. Holds up CAR-15. Lays it next to Catalina.

"She went for her gun." He nudges Red. Red nods.

Someone yells for ambulance. Another cop comes from bedroom. Carries two shoeboxes.

"Money's here."

Yes it is. Two hundred sixty-four thousand dollars. Counted last night. Laughing. Big fun.

Cops shout orders. Confusion. Laughter. All noise to Billy. Muted noise. Still deaf. He bleeds. Speckled buckshot wounds. Arm. Shoulder. Puts head on floor. Looks for Catalina's eyes.

"Catalina?" He implores. "Can you hear me?"

Cops roll her on her back. Her ribs just raw meat. One side of face dotted. Small bleeding holes. Opens her eyes.

"Billy...?" She whispers. Surprised. Then pain registers. "OH, I hurt like hell."

"They called for an ambulance."

She fades for a second. Tears in Billy's eyes.

"Billy don't go looking for payback."

"Sure."

"I know you. Promise."

"You got it."

She shudders. Gasps. Grits teeth. Low whine.

"AW, fuck it." She grunts. "Find 'em and waste their asses." She tries to laugh. Shudders again. Bites her lip.

"Who the fuck shot me?" she demands. "I wanna see his fucking face." Cops look at each other. Questioning. Red bends over her.

"Just take it easy ma'am. Doc's on the way."

She jerks forward. Spits on him. Big gob of blood, phlegm. Onto cop's chest. She falls back panting. Billy smiles.

"A pure mind fuck," she says. And dies.

Billy pounds his forehead into the floor. More cops crowd

room. Some yelling. Tossing bed. Tearing into closets. Dresser drawers dumped. Fridge emptied.

Billy starts thinking. Sees paperclip on floor. In front of face. Stretches. Eats it. And some dust bunny. Pockets clip in cheek.

Shoulder on fire. Cops flip Billy onto back. Paramedic examines Billy. "Nothing threatening," is the verdict. Looks at Catalina. "No hope here." Billy agrees. No hope there. Sees crochet needle. On floor. Near sofa.

"Can I sit him up?" Medic asks. Cop gives the okay. Paramedic helps Billy up.

Billy squirms. Like in pain. Maneuvering toward crochet needle. Sits on it.

Paramedic wipes away Billy's blood. Billy rears away. Like in pain. Grabs needle. Paramedic cleans, bandages shoulder. Billy withes a bit. Slides needle down butt crack.

"A doctor will have to remove this buckshot."

Shoulder throbs. Also neck. Billy blocks the pain. Stares at Catalina. Dead Catalina. Who dimed them? Who? Why? Why doesn't matter. Who does.

Billy put in squad car. Back seat. Rear windows half down. Hot as a blast furnace. No one cares. Not even Billy. Sits for hours. More cops come. Detectives. Cops grilling cops.

Billy waits. Planning.

Finally cops sit in front. Red and a Hispanic. Catalina's killer drives. They bullshit. Like Billy's not there.

"We drop numbnuts here off at the hospital wing, we go somewheres and get our story straight." Hispanic the boss. "You don't talk to no one 'til we get the story straight. Not even your fucking mother."

"Got it." Red nods. Nods too long.

Billy grabs needle from butt crack. Slides arms down past butt. Under ass. Behind knees. It hurts. Muscles strain. Something pulls in wounded shoulder. Pushes past pain. Gets cuffed hands to ankles. Takes a breath. Pushes arms. Lifts feet. Clears cuffs. Hands in front now.

Cops not paying attention. Concerned about own fate.

"Lawyer up. Union will give you one. Tell him same story. You know the drill. You interrogated enough perps. Just the straight story. Don't elaborate. She went for the gun. You shot. Her fault. You ID'd yourself. Warned her. Like 'Don't' some such shit. I yelled 'Gun!' and you shot. Everybody's got your back."

Billy slides needle under butt cheek. Spits paperclip into hand. Bent over so cops don't see. If watching. Not.

Billy knows cuffs. Bends wire. Inserts into cuff keyhole. Twists bent wire to eleven o'clock. If keyhole notch is six o'clock. Presses against internal ratchet. Click. Cuff loosens. Another click. More leeway.

Clicks too loud? Checks on cops. Nothing. Too much road noise with windows open. Cops talking like he isn't there. That's okay with Billy. That's great with Billy.

"Same story. Over and over. Every lawyer, and there will be a shitload of 'em. Every IA asshole. Your mom, your priest on your fucking deathbed when you're ninety-two fucking years old. Same fucking story. Got it?"

"Got it."

Cop car on Hollywood Freeway. Heavy traffic. Headed into city. Downtown. Can see towers in sea of smog.

Cuffs are off. Billy grabs needle. Not a needle. Crochet hook. Catalina corrected him. Catalina…

"Tell it like your favorite fucking joke. Same way every time. No elaboration. No bullshit. Don't go making new shit up just 'cause you're bored with it. You vary by a fucking word and the lawyers jump on that shit and beat you to death with it. Understand me?"

Billy leans forward. Left hand slides out window gap. Driver's window open too. No AC. Drives hook into Red's left ear. Punches through eardrum. Driver screams. Reaches for hook. Billy pounds needle with palm. Another three inches into Red's skull. More screams. Red grabs hook. Yanks. Hook snags on something. Red howls.

Hispanic draws pistol. Aims at Billy. Red loses control of car. Shrieks in pain. Hispanic fires. Car swerves. Window between seats shatters. Back windshield explodes. Billy deafened.

Hispanic aims again.

Car hits concrete median. Climbs wall. Up. Over. Flips. Car spins upside down. Another car hits. Skid across concrete. Metal screeches. Billy tumbles in back seat. Billy bounces. Car stops.

Billy smells gas. Steam billows. Engine still running. Revs. Billy crawls out back window. Glass embedded into arms, hands.

Walks to passenger side. Hispanic cop upside down. Hangs by seatbelt. Dazed. Still holds pistol. Billy takes. Redhead cop unconscious.

Traffic snarled. Half dozen crashes. Horns yelp. Billy hops median. Opposing traffic slowed. Rubberneckers. Billy steps in front of Mercedes. Waves gun.

"Out! Now!" Woman stops car. Climbs out. Weeping. Hands up. Billy slides behind wheel.

Drives away.

# CHAPTER ELEVEN

Downtown Los Angeles. Pershing Square. Tiny park. Habitat for winos, druggies and the insane. Raining. Across the street, Million Dollar Theater. Once a grand palace. Now showing low rent Mexican movies. Down the block, farmer's market. Indoor butcher stalls. Fruits and vegetable stands. Fresh fish. Narrow paths between the stalls. A maze.

Billy waits in a car. Watching. Stare unswerving. Rubs scars on shoulder. Buckshot bumps on neck. Speckled tattoo. Removed what he could with tweezers. Still hurts. The hurt helps him focus.

Eyes fixed on Checci. Shopping. New bodyguard carries bag. An apple here, an avocado there. At each stop vendor slips envelope into bag.

Checci limps. Wields cane. Ornate stick, silver handle.

Finishes rounds. Bodyguard pauses on sidewalk. Heavy rain. Bodyguard sprints across street. Into parking garage. Checci doesn't want to get wet. First mistake in two months.

Checci under awning. Alone.

* * *

Flood control basin. In the valley. Full of silt, refuse. Hardened mud, uprooted trees, brush. Assorted heavy equipment scattered about. Bulldozer, backhoe, woodchipper.

Rain stopped. Fog hangs over ground. Softens everything.

Billy parks. Checci spent night in trunk. Billy carries Checci's cane. Opens trunk. Checci blinks. Licks dry lips. Billy hauls him out. Dumps onto mud. Checci cuffed behind back. Needed paper clip. Billy laughs.

Billy pulls sword from cane. Pokes him.

"Who set me up?" Billy asks. Talks soft.

"You think I'm scared of that?" Checci spits. Dry mouthed. Not much moisture. "You think I don't know you're gonna kill me?"

"There's always hope," Billy whispers.

Billy drives a plotting stake into the mud. Five-pound sledge hammer. Found in Cat's toolbox. Clangs like a bell.

Uncuffs Checci. Cuffs hands in front. Checci doesn't fight it. Resigned. The hammer helps.

Hooks Checci's hands over stake. Grabs his ankles. Pulls straight. Sits on Checci's knees. Foot long screwdriver. Aimed at Achilles' heel. Pounds. Screwdriver punches through silk sock, flesh. Checci's good foot.

Checci screams.

Other foot kicks. Billy holds with knees. Screwdriver poised over second ankle. Pounds. Pierces. Both ankles skewered. Pounds screwdriver into hard mud. Deep.

Checci pinned to ground.

"Fuckyoufuckyoufuckyoufuckyou," Checci chants. He glares at Billy.

"Tell me," Billy demands. Whispers it into Checci's ear. Checci clamps jaw shut. Tough guy.

"You're gonna die," Billy tells him. "I can make you beg me to kill you."

"This ain't nothin'," Checci says.

"No, it isn't," Billy says.

Billy walks to the bulldozer. Climbs into the Cat's seat. Starts the engine.

Scouted the basin weeks before. Closed on weekends. Only chain-link fence to climb. Cut lock today. To drive through. Heavy machinery not locked. No need for keys. Wire easily available under dash. Hot-wired in no time. Practiced driving big Cat. No steering wheel. Control for right track, another for left. Stop one to turn, gun the other. Got the hang of it. Wasn't going to drive far. Always parked where he found it.

Checci stares up at him. Vague figure in the fog. Checci afraid now. Shouting. Billy can't hear over Cat's roar. Checci yells. Mouth moves. Neck muscles strain. Curses or pleas? Billy doesn't care.

Engages treads. A little power. Cat creeps forward. Clanking steel tracks. Inches forward.

Toward Checci's pinned feet.

Checci struggles. Futile. Stretched taut. Watches in terror. Eyes fixated. On left track. Rolling toward screwdriver. Poised over it. Then down. Over feet.

Billy hears Checci's scream over engine noise. Stops Cat. Lets engine idle. Steps down. Walks up to Checci.

Front of track nudges Checci's crotch. Below that legs are just chopped meat. Blood pooling.

Checci gasping for breath. Sucking air. Billy leans over.

"Sorry. Wanted to get only to the knees for the first step. Not enough practice time, I guess. I wonder how much this thing weighs. Suppose after a certain poundage it don't really matter. But you would know better than me."

Checci looking out of it. Billy slaps him. Hard.

"Focus. I think the next step is gonna really hurt. Crushing the pelvis. Turning your dick and balls to hamburger. But I think we'll wait a while, let this really sink in…"

"Kill me," Checci gasps.

"Tell me."

Checci smiles. "The brother."

Billy surprised. Confused. Then not. Checci's grin widens. "The Indian. Your whore's brother."

Billy hardens. Anger flares.

"He came to me," Checci says. Feeling in control.

Billy slaps him. "Bullshit."

"Okay. So I found him. Trying to sell my own shit. Put the word out. Knew they'd hit the street with it. Fucking amateurs."

A spasm of pain makes Checci strain. "It was the brother."

"Which one?" Billy asks. Anger cooling.

"Fuck if I know."

"Which one!?"

"I don't know. I don't remember. I...I couldn't tell the difference. Holy Mary, Mother of God..."

Billy raises the five-pound sledge. Checci fixes eyes on the steel head.

Billy brings it down. Checci's head caves.

Billy walks away. Into the fog.

* * *

Albuquerque. After six months. Searching. Two months in Santa Fe. South of Jicarilla Apache Reservation. Two months in Las Cruces. Outside Mescalaro Apache Reservation. Didn't know what kind of Apache the brothers were. More than one kind of Apache? Didn't know. Couldn't stake out reservation. White boy was the alien there. Small towns outside reservations just as bad. Strangers eyed with suspicion. Los Cruces and Santa Fe big enough. White man not noticed.

Cities were better. Easier to score drugs. Blue will show. Addicts have no choice.

Sets up easel in Santa Fe. Grew hair long. Hippie artist among hippie artists. Peasant shirt and beads. Knee length moccasins. Yellow aviator shades. Rusty VW van bought in Nevada.

Dug up money cache. Every robbery, every state hid bulk of

take at state line. Tape measure and Tupperware container. State line sign. "Welcome to…". Or "Thanks for visiting…". One hundred feet from most western or southern post of sign. Two feet down. Dug at night. Army entrenching tool. Bills stuffed into Glad freezer bags.

After L.A. escape dug up California. Nevada stash. After offing Checci retrieved Oregon-California North cache. Plenty of money. More out there. Enough to hunt.

Passed time in Santa Fe. Watercolors. Enjoyed painting. Made him see. But eyes always on street, pueblos. Ever searching. Waiting for brothers to come off reservation.

Day after day. No sigh. Nights cruising the streets. Nothing.

Los Cruces. Billy, new shades, ponytail now. Hand woven serape, smells of goat. Lays out blanket on sidewalk. Sells books. Paperbacks. Brautigan, Vonnegut, McPhee, Barthleme. Bought off hippie near college. Blanket and all. Moves about town. Watches drug sales. Patrols at night. Shelters. Liquor stores.

Works University area. Nothing. Old Messila courthouse. Tourist trap. Billy the Kid sentenced to hang here. Escaped. Watches San Albino church. Waiting for repentant brother maybe. To light candle for sister. Never happens.

Thinking brothers not around here. Maybe not even Apache. Just Indian wolf talk.

Tries Albuquerque. Adobe square. More New Mexico tourist flypaper. Old mission square. Quaint. Silver workers in windows. Indian women display silver and turquoise on blankets. Shops with rubber tomahawks. Kachina dolls. Japanese tourists burn Kodak, clickety, clickety, click.

Billy in jeans, jean jacket, old cowboy hat, beard. Wanders alleys and backstreets. Around Old Albuquerque. Not so quaint. Debris and garbage. Dirt streets. No sidewalks. Every step a dust cloud. Cracked walls. Busted windows. Graffiti.

Two months here. Ready to quit this. Re-think strategy. Back to Los Angeles?

Passes Indian Center. Used to be gas station. Awning, no pumps. Ghost of a sign. "Rowen's Texaco and Transmission." Hears a voice. Stops to peruse bulletin board. Next to open door. Cars and motorcycles for sale. Bands looking for musicians. Musicians looking for bands. Home massage. Babysitters. Opportunity to become millionaire working at home. Lost dogs.

Listens to voice inside.

"We must know how old you are." Delano talking to ancient Indian. Raisened skin. Milky eyes.

"The government will send me a present for my birthday?" Mummified Indian asks.

"Please think." Delano pleads. "This space must be filled in."

Delano waves form.

Inside a few used desks. Mismatched chairs. Copy machine. Young Indian women at most desks. Delano at biggest desk. Piled high with paperwork.

"There was a war. When I was born." Old man lisps. No teeth. "A great war, they said."

"This was when you were born?"

The old man nods slowly.

"Do you know who we were fighting?"

"We didn't fight." Old man shrugs. "It was a white man's war."

"Try to remember. Did you father tell you stories about this war?"

"Teddy Roosevelt fought."

"Hey!" Delano hollers. "Anyone know when the Spanish American War took place?"

Delano waits for a response. The women look at each other.

"1898, 1899." One of them. Chubby girl with glasses. "Maybe '97."

Delano shrugs. Fills in form. He looks up. Out the door. Billy turns away. Walks.

* * *

Delano first one in. Last one out. Every day. Helping Indian winos, elderly, teenage runaways, poor mothers, jobless. Redemption work? Billy doesn't care. Billy watches.

Delano closes shop. Late. Locks up. Walks to pick-up. Dodge Ram beater. Billy steps behind him. Hiding behind dumpster. Two-by-four to Delano's head. Thunk.

Delano wakes in a hole. Night. Moon overhead. Plywood walls. Four feet by four feet. Eight feet high. Rebar grid at bottom. Feet chained to rebar. Padlocked.

Delano knows where he is. Inside foundation form. Used to work construction. Sound of truck overhead. Fat rear of cement mixer loom over hole. Gravelly swish-swish, grind-grind of wet cement as barrel revolves.

Billy appears. Aims cement chute into hole. Leans down.

"Why'd you roll over on me and Catalina?"

Delano just blinks.

"Was it Blue?"

Delano stays silent.

"Your own fucking sister?"

Still nothing. Billy disappears. A clank. Cement starts to flow into pit. Delano backs away. Can't. Leans against wall.

Billy reappears.

"Why?"

"Money," Delano says. Watches cement creep up legs. Cold. "So you sold me."

"For a good price. The Wop wanted you bad."

Cement up to waist. Delano raises hands clear. Stares into Billy's eyes. "You loved her."

"I cried for her."

Cement reaches Delano's chest. Scared now. Cement rises to neck. Stretches his head. Strains to be taller.

"Who'll cry for you," Billy asks.

"It wasn't me! I wasn't me! It was Blue! He got...he..."

The cement reaches Delano's face. Billy tries to kick chute away. Too heavy. Dashes to switch. Yanks. Off! Back to hole.

Only Delano's hand shows. Billy reaches. Remembers Delano's chained feet. Digs for padlock key. Presses key into Delano's hand. Hand grasps key, goes under.

Billy waits. For a long time. Nothing moves. A bubble emerges from cement surface. Swells. Bursts.

* * *

Blue sits. Back against a dead tree. Brown paper bagged bottle between legs. Clothes filthy. Shiny with grime. Hair lank, matted. Mouth agape. Eyes seeing God. Maybe Usen.

Billy watches him. Inside a bar. Across the street. Through the front window. Plastic sunshade turns outside sepia. Like watching a movie.

When did Delano lie? When did he tell the truth? Was he lying to protect Blue. Then changed his mind. When death was close. Or lied trying to save his life?

The bar was cool. Outside an oven. Blue didn't seem to mind. Bundled in filthy layers. Blue doesn't seem to mind anything. Billy watched him get rained on. Watched mean sun bake Blue.

The bar was dark. A cave. Dusty floor. Dirty windows. Billy drinking Nehi. Chilled bottle. Cold makes teeth ache.

Men sat at bar. Cowboy boots. Straw hats. Nursing beers. Very little talk. TV on. No sound. No one watching.

Billy is tired. Beyond fatigue.

Two people enter bar. Blast of daylight blinds Billy. Glances at them. No threat. Woman and child. Billy contemplates bottle's sweat rings on tabletop.

What to do about Blue. Billy has a pistol in waistband. What to do.

Woman stands at door. Skinny. Dried up face. Child fresh

faced. Sad. What twenty years can do. Kid five or six. They walk to a booth. Man drinking shots. Billy watches.

"Jerry, it's time to go." Woman small voiced.

"One more." Man growls. "Told ya to wait in the car."

"It's hot in there," the boy whines.

"Jerry, you've had enough."

"Shut up bitch. You're embarrassing me."

"Jerry, please."

She is answered with a slap.

Everyone turns. Then turns back. Minding their own business.

The woman cries. Tears down her cracked skin. The boy sees his mother weeping. Begins to cry along.

"Stop yer bawlin', ya little snot."

The boy sniffles. Man grabs his ear, twists.

"Shut up!"

The boy squeals. Jerry backhands him.

Billy walks over.

"Don't do that," Billy says.

"Mind your own beeswax." The man looks at Billy. Acid washed blue eyes. Bloodshot. Tan line across forehead.

Billy shoots him.

One shot. Chest. Knocks Jerry back. He looks at Billy. Surprised. Starts to rise. Billy shoots him again.

The woman screams. Billy turns to the boy. Kid is stunned. Mother grabs boy. Wraps him. Protecting.

Billy looks around. Everyone stunned. So is Billy.

"Fuck," he says. To himself.

Bartender reaches under bar. Billy moves pistol bartender's way. Bartender changes his mind. Raises hands slow. Backs up.

Billy backs to front door. Eyes on the swivel.

Outside. Blinks in the sun glare. Steps to black Corvette. Drives off.

Past Blue. Blue is oblivious.

Billy drives north. Highway cleaves the desert. He drives fast. Top down. Hot wind dries his tears.

# CHAPTER TWELVE

Another bar. Billy's life. A history of bars. This one – Billy's bar. Actually, no name.

No sign out front. No phone listing. Just a bar. People knew about it. Enough. The Gringos' bar. If anything.

Another country. Mexico. U.S. border three hundred feet from Billy's window. He could see it. Watched it every day. Didn't cross. Not in years. But watched it. At his table. His back to the wall. Drinking.

Started drinking. Drunk for three months. From bar to bar. Zaragoza, Galeana, Ascension, Palomas. Woke up in this one. Owner a lunger. Looking to sell. No buyers.

Billy sobered up. Enough to venture back north. Dug up caches. Seven states worth. Maybe more out there. Couldn't remember. Bought the bar. And drank.

Not drunk no more. But never sober. Cultivated a haze. A numbness. Deadened.

Put in a whore. Upstairs. Next to his room. Put in a jukebox. Downstairs. Played music he liked. Fuck everybody else. All American music. Fuck 'em.

Had his favorites memorized. Lifted the top. Punched free play button. Richie Havens doing Dylan. Perfect.

Played the jukebox. Drank. Watched the border. Reads. Books he already read. Travis McGee, Dash Hammett, Ross Thomas.

"Got the cases all stacked." Jorge. Fifteen. Odd job boy. A long line of boys. This one eager.

Billy nods.

"Drain on the ice machine is clogged again," Billy tells him.

"Shit. Okay. After lunch?"

Billy nods.

"Want something?" Jorge asks.

Billy shakes his head. Hardly eats. Skinny now. Meat, bone and sinew. Eyes sunken. Looks like that lunger. Maybe it's the bar. Haunted, he heard one of the whores say.

"Inez!" Jorge calls out. "Lunch! Edgar?"

Inez looks up from her magazine. Soap opera stars. Pretty but plump Inez.

"Where you going?" she asks.

"Colonel Sanders?" Edgar suggests. Old man. A regular. Dyed hair pitch black. Dyed mustache. Surface of the moon acne scars.

Jorge collects money and orders.

Billy watches him go. Little Honda 90. Kicks up rooster tail of dust. Dusty worm hangs in the air. No wind. Just heat. Billy keeps the bar cold.

Caddy crosses border. Big pink land yacht. Convertible. Top up. Three men.

Approaches slow. Parks out front. Three sets of eyes contemplate bar. One slips a hand under jacket. Scratches armpit. Jacket in this heat?

They enter bar. Cowboys. Boots. Croc and snake. Fancy belts. Big belt buckles. Cowboy hats. Feathered hat bands. Leather vest with conchos. Suede jacket, arrow pockets. Levi jacket, brand new. Drugstore cowboys. Boots never touched horseshit. They swagger. Strut. Big dick walk.

"Who owns this here roach trap?" Leather vest stares down

Edgar. Edgar stone faces it. Seen it all. This, too. Survived them all.

"I do." Billy speaks soft. But they hear. Leather Vest walks over. Cowboy heels hard on floor. Other two bracket Leather Vest. Leather Vest sits at Billy's table. Other two sit.

"We get us something to drink here?" Suede Jacket demands. Doesn't ask. These types never ask. Billy sees hint of leather under armpit.

"Stupid question number one," Billy says, nods to Edgar. Leather Vest doesn't like smart ass answer. But laughs anyway. Polite bastard.

"Three beers. None of that Mexican coon piss. And make them fucking cold." Suede Jacket calls out.

Levi Jacket eyes Inez. She crosses her legs. Shows some thigh. Reflex. Never hurts to advertise.

Edgar puts three Buds on the bar. Clunk. "Beers up!"

"Well, bring 'em over here, boy." Suede jacket calls. "Didn't figure this was some kinda self service."

Inez grabs the bottles. Totes them over. Leans over. Demonstrates cleavage. Grand Canyon cleavage.

Billy just watches Leather Vest. Suede Jacket's itchy armpit.

Levi passes around beers. Smiles at Inez. Wolf teeth grin. "Thanks brown eyes."

"You like my eyes?" Inez working it.

Levi sticks finger out. Pulls down blouse elastic. Peers into valley of breasts.

"I love your eyes." Levi laughs at own joke. Inez removes his hand. Playful like. "Cost you a dollar to look." Inez all coy.

"What'll I get for twenty?"

"More than you can handle." She sashays away. A pro. "For thirty dollar, heaven on earth."

Levi turns to Leather Vest. "Sarge?"

"Sure Cecil. Wet that wick."

"Pussy hound." Suede growls.

Levi/Cecil stands. Wraps arm around Inez. "Where we do this?"

"I got a room upstairs." She leads him by the hand.

Leather Vest gets to business.

"Richie Reyes said you could introduce us to some interesting people."

"He did?" Billy rises. Walks to bar. Leather Vest and Suede follow. Billy steps behind bar. They try to go with. Edgar blocks them. Leather Vest shrugs. They take stools.

Billy dials the phone.

Jorge returns. Three KFC boxes. Passes one to Edgar.

"Where's Inez?"

Edgar points to ceiling.

"Her chicken'll get cold." Jorge opens his own.

"She won't be hungry." Leather Vest leers. "She's getting' a healthy hunk of tube steak."

He and Suede dirty laugh. Jorge sets his jaw. Takes a stool far away. Edgar eats chicken. Billy stays near horse's cock shotgun under bar.

Answering machine picks up. Billy dials another number.

Suede squints at Jorge.

"These greasers don't got no sense of humor 'less they's settin' dogs afire or somethin'."

"Reyes." Filtered voice on phone.

"Three men here," Billy tells the phone. "Cowboys. Leather Vest, Mister Suede and the boy from Levi's."

"Sarge and Cecil," Leather Vest says.

"Joe Tarpsman," Suede says.

"I don't want to hear no fucking last names," Billy barks.

Tells phone, "Sarge, Cecil and some asshole."

"You know what they say." Reyes laughs. "The bigger the buckle, the tinier the dick. One of them gringos got a tattoo on his left arm? A skull, 'Born To Lose'? Ain't that the fucking truth. The fucker wearing suede. In this heat."

Billy grabs Suede's left arm. Slides up the sleeve. Tat like Reyes says. Crude. Prison probably.

"Oh, shit," Leather Vest says. "Almost forgot. Bartender, a bag of them peanuts."

Edgar tosses. Leather Vest catches. Pockets.

"They been bonafided?" Billy asks phone.

"As best can be done. They were regulars of Garcia's. Not no more. Garcia got dead."

"Garcias's dead?" Billy didn't know. "Hazard of the job."

"Not this kind of dead." Reyes laughs. Reyes good natured. Unless crossed. "Garcia got drunky. Passed out in a puddle on the way home. Drowneded. In, like, three inches of water. Ain't that a bitch."

"Stupid way to die."

"Tell me a smart one." Reyes hangs up.

Billy hangs up. Leather Vest grins.

"Now can we do some business?" he asks. "You tell your people that I don't want no boo. Just the nose candy. I got me one hundred and eighty large and I expect—"

"Shut the fuck up."

Billy smiles. "I don't talk deal. I don't do your business for you. I just set you up with a meet with the people who do."

"Okay, okay. Swear to Christ, you people got more middlemen than the fucking government. Should have known you weren't the main man."

A feral grin. Waiting for Billy to snap at the bait. Join the wolf talk. Billy considers it. He doesn't like Leather Vest. But he doesn't like a lot of people. Wants to go back to his window. His drink. His numbness. Leather Vest making him feel something. Pissed off. But it's still a feeling.

Leather Vest waiting. Wants to go fist city. Billy doesn't use his hands. Sawed off does the work for him. Doesn't have to decide.

Inez comes tumbling down the stairs. Rolling. Bumpety-bumpety-bump. Half wrapped in a sheet.

"Bitch!" Levi's/Cecil comes after. Shirt open. Belt flapping. Fly at half-mast.

"Come back here you goddamned whore!"

Inez catches herself halfway down stairs. Levi's/Cecil kicks her. She tumbles rest of the way. Thumpity-thump-thump. Sprawls. One tit out. Curses him in Spanish.

"Stupid cunt." Levi's/Cecil spread eagled over her. "I paid for that hole. I can do whatever the fuck I want with it."

Levi/Cecil bends down. Slaps her. Once. Twice. First in the face. Second in the tit. Inez squeals. Curls up. Ducks the next blow.

Jorge rushes over. Grabs Levi's/Cecil's slapping arm. Suede dropkicks Jorge. Nut kick. From behind. Jorge collapses. Clutches nuts. Vomits KFC and Coca-Cola.

Levi's/Cecil and Suede kick at boy.

SNAP-SNAP. Everyone freezes. Everyone knows that sound. Shotgun round being chambered. Edgar aims sawed off pump. The cowboys stare. Shotgun muzzle big as 55-gallon drum.

"You want to ease up on my employees," Billy says, quietly.

"Leave the greaser, boys." Leather Vest orders. Turns to Billy. "When we getting' our business rollin'?"

"We'll be at the Best Western. White side of the border." The cowboys amble toward the door. Suede walking backward. Hand aimed at armpit.

"Hold it," Billy says. Again quietly.

The three stop. Six eyes on the shotgun.

"You owe me," Billy says. "For the beers."

"And the peanuts," Edgar adds.

Leather Vest sneers. Pulls out wallet. Chained to his belt. Withdraws a bill. Balls it up. Tosses it at Billy.

"And I'll take a Coke to go." Smiles. Friendly smile. Evil intent in eyes. Billy grabs Coke from cooler under bar. Tosses it to him.

Leather Vest catches. Mister Cool. Two finger salute. Saunters out. Other two follow.

Billy waits. Give them time to change their mind. Muster some courage. Load their guns.

Engine starts. Billy watches Caddy roll past window.

Turns to Inez, Jorge. Boy's eyes filled with hate. Some directed at Billy. You're responsible, those eyes say.

* * *

Six hours to mull it over. Six hours at the window. Jorge stewing in his own juices. Getting drunk. Fueling a fire with Tequila. Inez watches her brother. Worried.

She joins Billy. Bump on her forehead. Cut on her chin. Lip swollen. Holding ice to it.

"You must stop him." She whispers. "He is talking crazy talk."

Billy doesn't answer. Doesn't look her way. Semi-truck passes through border crossing. Then a van. A car full of college kids. Box truck.

"You can stop him." She won't go away.

Billy watches bus come through. Migrant workers. Inez slaps back of his head. He looks at her. He can take a hint.

"Look at me when I talk! This is important! He will be killed or he will kill somebody. Just as bad. I still die inside. He is my brother. Do something."

"None of my business."

"It is business. I am business."

"I rent you a room. You're a convenience for the customers. Like the jukebox. Or the toilet."

She takes it. Tears in her eyes.

"We are family. Me, my brother, Edgar. And you. We take care of each other," Billy turns back to his window.

"I have no family," he says. "I don't need a family."

She turns away. Disgusted. Walks to the stairs. Limping. Jorge watches her. Looks at Billy. Joins Billy at the window.

"Women." Jorge slurring. "Do not unnerstan' what men mus' do, you know."

Drunken bravado. Billy has seen it before. Too many times. Gets men beat. Cut. Shot. Dead.

"I mus' regain my honor." Jorge raises his chin. Proud. "The honor of my sister."

"Your sister is a whore." Billy lays it out. "There's no honor there."

"Revenge then."

"Revenge is for suckers."

Billy drinks deep. Remembering.

"I have no honor because I let my sister be a whore? Maybe so. But I don' need to hear this shit from you. You have no honor. You have no balls. You are a dead man."

Jorge reaches across the table. Taps Billy on the forehead.

"Behind your eyes there is no life."

What is it today? Everybody touching him. Billy drinks. '70 El Camino crosses border. Candy apple green paint job. Good chrome.

Jorge pulls out his knife. Switch blade. Chrome dragon on the handle. Blade comes straight out of handle. Not sideways. Dog's dick.

"I will take my honor. The man will suffer."

"There are three of them."

"I only want the one who beat on my sister. Mano a mano."

"Take the shotgun."

"It must be close. It is personal. A knife is more honorable."

"Bullshit."

"I do not expect you to understand. You have no honor."

"You said that."

Jorge turns and leaves.

* * *

Billy sleeps very little. Short naps. Day or night. Lays in bed. Mind adrift. Pushing away bad memories. Clinging to the good. There are few. But cherished.

Endless strings of sleepless nights.

Three in the morning. Reading. Twain. All of Twain. Again.

BAM! BAM! BAM! Pounding on wood. Downstairs door. Billy is startled. Grabs .45 off nightstand.

BAM! BAM! Billy rises. Walks barefoot. Out of bedroom. Down hall. Past Inez at her door. Eyes swollen. Crying all night.

"Stay here," he tells her. Down the stairs.

BAM! BAM! BAM! Door shudders under each blow.

"I'm coming, goddamnit." Floor cold on feet. Inez bumps into his back.

"Stay here!" He yells at her. Pushes her back. She falls on her ass. Bad day for Inez.

A car engine heard. Going away.

Billy walks across bar. Reaches front door. Pauses. Slips the bolt. Unsnaps lock. Opens door.

Jorge a bundle on the entry.

Dead. Bloodied head hangs. Neck limp. Shirt blood soaked. Cut and sliced. Dragon knife pokes out of chest.

Billy steps outside. Cool breeze tonight. Nothing moves on the street. Border crossing lit up. Nothing moves but bugs kamikazeing the lights. Nobody on the street.

Billy steps back inside. Finds Inez in middle of bar. Transfixed. Slow, soft groan of pain escapes her lips. Volume increase. A wail. A scream.

* * *

Billy at his window. Inez sits with him. Both drinking.

"I hate God," she says. "I hate gringos. I hate you."

Billy listens. Least he could do.

"Jorge had dreams. We were saving our money. We..."

"He was the lucky one," Billy says. To himself. But aloud. Inez curls her lip.

"I hate you most of all."

"So do I."

"You don't even care I hate you. What is wrong with you?"

Billy watches. Out his window. The Caddy crosses the border. Pulls up. Parks. Cowboys climb out.

"Go upstairs," he tells Inez.

"I don't take orders from you. I am not afraid of them. Like you."

"Be afraid of me, then. Go…up…stairs. Now."

Something in his eyes. Scares her. She walks away. Climbs stairs.

The cowboys enter. Billy stays at his boot at window.

Leather Vest approaches Billy. Suede keeps hand under coat.

"We best have us an understanding, bud," Leather Vest tells Billy. "The little door porch present you found this morning, it don't have nothing to do with our business."

"You gonna get me a new errand boy?"

"The boys were partying too hard. Things got out of hand."

Billy nods. Suede takes hand out of jacket.

"Your people sit over there." Billy points across bar. Three well dressed Mexicans sit. Bar is empty otherwise. Edgar on his perch. Other trade discouraged. They understand.

"Glad you're the sensible type." Leather Vest nods. Tips cowboy hat. Turns to Levi's/Cecil. "Get me a Coke. And a bag of peanuts."

Levi's/Cecil walks over to fetch. Suede and Leather Vest join the Mexicans.

Billy's glass is empty. Takes gun from lap. Pockets it. Automatically fills his glass. Tequila. Billy hates the taste.

Billy sips. Eyes stairs.

"She'll get over it," Edgar says. "She's young."

"And we're not," Billy says. Edgar grins. Gold tooth. Hardly ever shows it.

Levis/Cecil takes Coke and peanuts. Joins partners.

Billy and Edgar watch negotiations. Done very quiet. Very cool. Discreet.

Nods and scraping of chairs. They all stand. Deal done. Walk to door. One Mexican approaches Billy. Hands him folded money. Held with rubber band. Billy nods. Pockets it. Next to gun. Counting it would insult. Dishonorable, Billy says to self.

"Much grass, as the gringos say." Mexican grins. Twisted by cleft palate scar.

"Mucho gracias to you, too," Billy says. Mexican smiles.

The Mexicans leave.

Leather Vest walks to Billy.

"I hear there's a service charge for the how-de-do."

"Five hundred dollars."

"Jesus." From Levi's/Cecil.

"That's a big ol' hunk of change for a coupla phone calls." Suede complains.

Billy sees something. Cowboys have backs to stairs. At the top, Inez. Pistol in hand. Nickel-plated automatic.

Billy turns away from her. Smiles at Leather Vest.

"Try to do it yourself." Tells Leather Vest, "Use the Yellow Pages. I don't give a fuck. You pay me or you get no deal. Now. Or ever again this side of the border."

Leather Vest sets down Coke, pockets peanuts. Thinks. Reaches for chained wallet. Finds and slides five bills across bar.

Billy takes it. Counts them. Slowly. Leather Vest stews. Billy glances at Inez. Her hands shake.

Billy pockets the hundreds. Keeps hand in pocket, next to gun. Waiting for Inez. Will she do it?

Leather Vest heads to door. Billy stops him. Giving Inez her chance.

"And your bar bill," Billy says.

"What?"

"Coke and a bag of peanuts."

"Fuck you."

"That's the way you want to play it."

And the cowboys leave. Never aware of Inez. And her gun. Amateurs. Billy looks at her. Her arm drops. Gun hangs limp.

"Who were you gonna shoot?" Billy asks. "Me or them?"

"All of you."

Billy laughs. First time in a long time. Inez flees to her room. Door slams behind her.

Billy walks to his window. Caddy tows a plume of dust behind it. Disappears behind the yellow cloud. Billy watches until the dust settles. Puts on his jacket. Army fatigue jacket. Big pockets. Comfy. Jungle weight. Perfect for hot weather. Still has unit patch from Nam. 173rd. 'The Rock.' Name patch torn off. U.S. Army tag ripped off. Leaving darker green over pockets. Loves this jacket. From when he knew what he was supposed to do.

Finally turns. Walks to the bar. Takes the shotgun. Checks the magazine. Five rounds. Enough.

Edgar watches. Frowns.

Billy sticks sawed off into paper bag. Heads for the door. Stops short. Turns. Unclips key ring. Tosses keys to Edgar.

Edgar wants to say something. Billy winks at him.

Edgar grows a smile. Smile fades before Billy is out the door.

Billy takes a cab. Always one at the border crossing. Stops cab a block from the warehouse. Where the deal always goes down.

Pink Caddy parked across street. Next to Range Rover with Mexican plates.

Boy slouches next to warehouse door. Thirteen maybe. Skinny. Flipping kitchen knife at plywood sheet. Wood chewed to splinters.

Boy eyes Billy. Brown paper bag in Billy's fist. Suspicious. Paid to be.

"I came to see Esteban," Billy tells him. "There's gonna be trouble. Go home."

Boy hesitates. Balances knife on one finger. Frowns at Billy. Eyes paper bag.

"Go home." Billy growls. Boy jumps. Runs. Dust explodes with every step.

Warehouse is dark inside. The three Mexicans and three cowboys bracket a table. Table is a door astride two sawhorses.

One Mexican counts money. One stands guard, machine gun at ready. Esteban watches. El Jefe.

Leather Vest watches Suede check out dope. Plastic baggies. Tongue and test tube tests. Every bag. Levi's/Cecil on guard duty. Long barreled Ruger .44.

Billy approaches. Shotgun in one had. Pistol in other. No one notices. Not at first. Concentrating on deal. Bad watch outs.

Billy gets close. Close enough.

"Anyone moves, he dies."

That gets their attention. They freeze.

Billy steps into shaft of sunlight. Sun pours through hole in the roof. Dust motes dance around Billy's head. He glows. Steps back into the shadows.

"This some kind of set up?" Leather Vest glares at Esteban. "You boys trying to burn me?"

"You owe me, cowboy," Billy tells him. "A Coke and a bag of peanuts."

"Is he crazy?" Leather Vest asks anyone.

"Yes, I think so." Esteban looks disgusted. He knows. This is turning to shit. "Give him his money."

Leather Vest purses his lips. Doesn't move.

"I will pay," Esteban says. Trying to save his deal. His life. He knows. "Billy here."

Esteban nervously tosses wad of cash at Billy. Lands at Billy's feet. Cloud of dust mushrooms as it lands.

"No," Billy says. "From his pocket."

Esteban sighs. Leather Vest nods. Made a decision.

"I'm reaching for my wallet. Nothing else." Leather Vest

reaches behind his back. Real slow. Levi's/Cecil raises the Ruger. Billy sees him. Smiles.

"No," Esteban says. Like a prayer. Soft.

Leather Vest dives for the floor. Billy fires. Levi's/Cecil first. Then machine gun Mexican. Levi's/Cecil back flips. Load of double odd into the chest. Machine gun Mexican spins. Suede reaches. Shot. Other Mexican tries. Shot.

Machine gun fires into roof. Light stabs bullet holes overhead. More dust falls. Gun smoke and dust. Instant fog. Big noise.

Billy puts another into machine gun Mexican. Shotgun empty.

Silence.

A body moves. Billy drops shotgun. Trades for pistol. Someone cries. Someone prays in Spanish.

Billy walks among the dead. The wounded. Removes guns. Throws them into dark.

Esteban is alive. Hurt? Just playing possum? Billy reaches Leather Vest. Both knees are hamburger. Bloody. Caught in crossfire?

Billy kicks him. He gasps in pain. Alive. Billy reaches down. Pips wallet from back pocket. Rips chain from belt loop. Flips wallet open.

"A buck twenty-five. American. I'm taking two." Does that. "The difference is for my trouble."

Drops wallet. Rips open front pocket. Billy takes car keys.

Steps on Leather Vest's left wrist. Aims pistol. Fires round into palm.

Leather Vest screams.

"Other hand," Billy orders.

Billy steps off left wrist. Leather Vest cradles it to his chest. "Other hand," Billy says again. Leather Vest whimpers. "Aw, fuck it." Billy shoots him. In the heart.

"Fuck it all." Billy walks away.

"Why?'

Billy turns. Esteban rises from floor. One bloody shoulder. Asking. "Bored," Billy says, then, "Tired."

Somebody hit Billy. In the back. With a baseball bat. Hard. His back is numb. But…blood on his stomach.

He rises. How did he get on his knees? He turns.

The skinny Mexican kid. Holding a revolver. In both hands. The Ruger. Kid shocked. At what he's done. At what might happen.

Billy raises his pistol. Arms moves slow. Gun is suddenly heavy. Air like syrup. Kid drops Ruger. Runs.

Billy tries to walk. He can. He hears laughter. Turns. Esteban. Grinning. Laugh becomes cough.

Billy walks out. Sun hits him like a hot slap. Looks around. Nothing moves but the dust.

Opens Caddy door. Eases behind the wheel. "The peanuts made me thirsty."

A boy's head. Pops over back seat. Blond, blue eyed. Six or seven. Holds Coke bottle.

Billy pokes ignition with key. Fingers slippery with blood. "Where's my daddy?"

# CHAPTER THIRTEEN

"You stealing our car?" the kid asks. Peanut crumbs around mouth.

"No," Billy says. Pauses. How to say it. "Your daddy won't be coming back."

"How will I get home?"

Billy starts the car. Drives.

His bar on the way. Billy slows. Inez at the window. His window. They see each other.

Billy stomps on the gas. Border crossing ahead. Doesn't slow. Busts right through cross bar. Passes car at gate.

Checks rear view mirror. Border guard on his walkie-talkie.

Billy puts two spare clips on seat.

"I'm thirsty." Boy climbs over front seat. Billy pushes him back.

"Stay in the back seat. Put your seatbelt on."

The kid obeys.

Billy sees flashing lights in rear view mirror. New Mexico State Police. Coming up fast. Pulls alongside. Cop riding shotgun motions Billy to pull over.

Billy gives him the finger. Jerks thumb at back seat.

Cop looks. Sees kid.

Billy stands on the gas pedal. That hurts. Caddy pulls ahead. Cops drop behind.

Somewhere in the desert. Another cop car joins. Then another. Taking a curve Billy sees four cruisers now. Keeping their distance. Later a helicopter overhead. Chopper's shadow races alongside Caddy.

Hot dry air buffets Billy's face. Boy sits up front. When did he do that? Kid plays with pistol magazine. Takes bullet out. Billy snatches magazine away. Let's boy play with bullet.

Billy's mind going foggy. Boy turns on radio. Cruising stations. Preachers. Muzak. Mexican polkas. Then the Who. "Behind Blue Eyes."

"Leave it there," Billy tells him.

Boy turns up the volume. Billy tries to sing along. Voice is hoarse. Kid joins in. Grinning. Billy smiles back.

Checks speedometer. Ninety plus. Gas gauge. Nosing empty.

Gas station ahead. Billy slows. Pulls into station. Misjudges. Too fast. Slams on the brakes. Caddy skids to a hard stop. That hurts.

Dust rises. Settles. Billy backs to pump. Attendant saunters out.

"Whoa there mister. 'Bout tore out my bell hose."

Old skinny wrinkled man. Dried up by the desert. Stands next to pump. Billy points pistol at him.

"Fill 'er up."

"Yessir!" Old man goes scared. Grabs nozzle. Opens gas cap. Reflex. Never takes eyes off Billy. Not Billy, Billy's gun.

"You don't have to point that at me, ya know."

"I don't tell you how to pump gas, you don't tell me how to rob."

"I got to pee." Boy squirms in his seat.

"Step out of the car. Do it right there. Piss on a tire," Billy tells him.

"Really?"

Kid seems thrilled. Naughty.

"Sure. You never know what kind of germs you're gonna find in a public toilet."

Billy watches the kid pee. Painting the tire. Experimenting. An artist.

State Police helicopter hovers overhead. Rattling the air. Four cop cars wait down the road. Billy digs in glove box. Pulls Caddy's registration. Leather Vest was Roger. Last name Sergeant. Home in Albuquerque.

Attendant glances at the cruisers.

"Don't hurt me." Old man's voice cracks. "I'm just some poor fucker working for the minimum wage."

Billy dips into his pocket. It hurts. Pulls a wad of bills. Bloody mess. Tosses it to attendant.

"Get the kid a Coke."

Machine stands by the door. Horizontal coffin cooler. Bottles hang is freezing water. Billy would like that. Freezing water. Cool the fire in his gut.

"Dr Pepper," kid says. "I like Dr Pepper. Daddy always gets me Coke but I like Dr Pepper."

"You heard him."

Old man walks to machine. Feeds it change. Brings over two Dr Peppers. Kid rushes to get them. Hurries back to car. Pump clicks. Tank full. Attendant rushes to yank nozzle.

Billy steers back onto highway. The parade resumes. Boy opens bottle. Snaps cap off on glove compartment door. Done this before.

"Want some?" Kid offers a bottle.

Billy thirsty. But it hurts to swallow spit. Shakes his head. Kid puts extra bottle into cup holder. Looks back at cop convoy.

"Are we the good guys or the bad guys?" Kid asks, drinks.

"You pick."

Billy and the kid. Singing along with the radio. Bobby Fuller Four, "I Fought The Law."

"And the law won…" Billy laughs through the pain.

Albuquerque ahead. Billy pulls out map. Takes next exit. Follows the map. Gets lost. Hard to think clearly.

Finds the street. Jackson. Just like all the others. Number 4203. Pulls into driveway. Waits. Sees blood pool on floor. Steam rises from Caddy hood. Temp gauge red lined.

Cops already down at next corner. Must have traced plate. Leaves engine running.

Roadblock cops stand behind vehicles. Guns ready. Parade fills other end of street. Cops bail. Take positions.

"We're here!" Kid yells. Startles Billy. Raises pistol reflexively.

"That's where I live! That's my house!"

The front door opens. Woman steps out. Short. Big tits, big ass. Small waist. Dyed red hair. Roots showing. Frowns at Billy. Sees kid.

"Squirt?"

"Hi, mama!"

She approaches Caddy. Looks at police barricades. Stares at Billy.

"They wanted to put an officer in the house," she tells Billy. "But I wouldn't let them."

Billy steps out. The pain blossoms. Starts in belly, streams through arms, legs. Head woozy. Seat sticky with blood. She sees Billy's wound. His pistol. Backs off a step. He winces.

Kid climbs out. Mother rushes to son. Boy leaps into her arms. Billy watches. Another pain blossoms.

"Into the house," Billy tells her. Follows them inside.

It is cool in the house. AC cranking. Nice.

Super clean house. Lots of knick-knacks. Doilies.

The woman hugs her boy. Kisses his head. Kid ducks some. She looks past the kid to Billy. Afraid.

"I'm hungry," kid says.

Woman tries to laugh. It dies quickly.

"Go and fix yourself some Sugar Smacks." Boy runs off. Billy and the woman. Look at each other. Both calculating.

"You're hurt."

"I didn't notice."

"My husband. He dead?"

Billy nods. Walks to windows. Checks. Cops staying in place.

"Good. I'm free."

Billy looks at her, surprised.

Phone begins to ring. Woman goes for it.

"Leave it."

She backs off.

"What do you want?" she asks.

What does he want? He thinks on it.

"Out."

"Where you going?"

"Far as I can." Checks windows again. Phone keeps ringing. Irritating.

"Pull the cord on that thing will ya."

She does. Phone rings somewhere else in house. Muted. Better.

Steps into dining room. Leather Vest did okay. Roger. Sees gun case. Opens it. Model 94 Winchester. Twenty-two Remington. Mosby shotgun. AR-15, civilian M-16. Billy knows the weapon.

Takes it. Ammo drawer. Three loaded magazines. Banana clip. Pockets them.

"I need some wheels. Caddy's overheating."

"There's a pick-up in the garage."

Windows again. Police move down the street. Slowly. By the numbers. Cover and run. Cover and run. Working toward the house.

"Cops in the garage too?"

"If they are I didn't put them there."

"Show me."

Leads him into kitchen. Boy at the table. Pouring milk into bowl. Looks at Billy, at mom.

"We're outlaws."

"There's blood on your shirt," she tells boy. "After you eat, bath time. And clean clothes."

Her voice is curt. Seems on the verge of tears. Takes a breath. Pulls herself together. Grabs keys from rack by door. Turns to Billy.

"Thank you. I love him."

Billy is mesmerized by kitchen. A whole other world. He remembers a kitchen. Blood on the floor.

She opens garage door. Dark inside. Billy's eyes search. Outside door closed. Hot rod pick-up. Big tires. Jacked cab. Billy circles it. Pushes woman in front of him. Garage super clean. Like house.

Kneels down. Pain makes him gasp. Looks under pick up. Nothing. Rises. The pain repeats. Staggers. Woman catches. He pulls away. Leans against truck. Gets his strength back. Holds hand out. She passes him keys.

Billy climbs up into cab.

"Go back to the kitchen."

"You're not going to use me as a hostage?"

"You volunteering?"

She dashes back into kitchen. Boy in doorway. Eating cereal. Mom yanks him back. Slams door. Lock clicks.

Billy starts up engine. Big block roars. Slides shift into reverse. Manual. Backs up to garage door. Presses against it. Feathers the gas, clutch.

Slams into first. Stomps on it.

Tires squeal on concrete floor. Smoke. Grab traction.

Truck leaps.

Smashes through garage back wall. Truck leaps across back yard. Past swing set. Smashed barbecue. Eight-foot redwood fence.

Man climbing fence. All in black. SWAT in white letters across back. Fence shatters into kindling. Cop rolls across hood, away.

Two starbursts appear in windshield. Police snipe on neighbor's roof. Billy gets a glimpse of sniper. Bullets ping against car body.

Cuts across new yard, down driveway. Sideswipes Toyota. Crosses street.

Another driveway. Another fence. Another yard. Barely misses pool. A new fence. Low chain link. Bottom gives. Fencing claws furrows over hood, up windshield. Another yard, acres of grass. Tears ruts into lawn.

Bounces into empty street. Billy speeds away. No police to be seen. Muted sirens.

Billy drives. Checks gauges. No trouble. Bullets didn't hit anything vital.

Highway. Street roads. Residential. Industrial. Five-lane. Two-lane. Dirt roads. Just drives.

No destination. Driving skills deteriorating. Weaving from shoulder to shoulder. Barely keeping truck between the ditches.

Sweat dripping down face. Helicopter slaps air overhead. Billy drowns it with radio. Loud. Jackson Brown, "The Pretender".

*** * ***

Billy wakes. Blacked out. How long? Pick-up nudging a big rock. In gear. Lurching forward.

A sign. "No trespassing without permission." Warnings from U.S. Government. From Reservation authorities.

Billy steps out. Falls out. Pain wakes him. Surveys pueblo. Towering city into rock cliff. Adobe huts stacked like kids blocks.

Looks back. Tire tracks in wave pattern across sand. Dust clod in distance. Flashing lights from cop cars.

Music on truck radio. Poco, "Crazy eyes." Likes that song.

Thunder in the distance. Helicopter high overhead. Caravan of cops approaching. Dozen vehicles. Maybe more.

Billy grabs AR-15. Examines it. Not AR. Full M-16. Illegal. But full auto.

Billy trots to base of pueblo. Bent over. Hurts big time. Deep in his gut.

Steps carved into face of cliff. He climbs.

Lead cop car skids to stop. Thirty meters back. Cop leans on door. Aims rifle. Pops off five shots.

Bullet chip stone below Billy. Walk their way up. Ricochet hits Billy in calf. He stumbles.

Billy turns. Fires M-16. Hits the cop car. Shatters windshield. Cop ducks.

Billy continues climbing steps. More cars arrive.

Two cops sprint to pueblo. Billy empties rest of magazine. They rush back behind cars.

Billy staggers through village. Walks and climbs. The high ground. Always take the high ground. A dog ambles over, sniffs at him. Wanders away.

Billy climbs steps. Ladders. Oblivious.

Reaches top of pueblo. Can see for miles. The Who. Desert below. Cars and men.

He sways. Dizzy. Drops down. Lays back. Stares at the sun. Beginning to set. Slipping below the mountain. Getting out while the getting is good. Don't blame the sun.

Billy waits.

The ladder to rooftop trembles. Billy fires a short burst. Bullets chew ladder top.

"Take the ladder away!" Billy yells.

Ladder slips down. Gone.

Sun disappears. Night. Cold. Billy lays on warm roof. Holding the day's heat. Stares at night sky. So many stars salt the night.

He listens. Night birds. Cop radio traffic.

He peeks. Cops settled in. A tent even. Work lights. Cops mill around.

Footsteps below him. He ducks back. Object flies up from below. Rattles across rooftop. A canteen. Clatters to a stop.

"Some water for you." Voice calls out. "Sheriff Cleon here. What's your name pilgrim?"

"That's as good as any."

Silence for a while. Billy drinks. Hurts deep. Gut shot. Not a good idea. But mouth dry. Checks leg wound. Bleeding's stopped.

"Why you come here?" Voice echoes out of ladder hole.

"This is where I stopped."

Another long silence. Billy hears murmur of voices. Shuffling of feet. Clank of equipment belts. Coughs. Smells cigarette smoke.

"Pilgrim? You still there?"

"I stepped out for dinner but I'm back now."

"You hungry?"

Billy doesn't answer. His guts throb. Pain spreading across his body. Rises and falls. With every breath. Pain pulses. Every beat of his heart.

"Listen here Pilgrim. I know you're hurtin'. Left a lake of blood in your ride. Looks like someone was slaughterin' a hog in there. The Caddy, too. How 'bout we call off the whole shebang? Truck you on down to a hospital?"

Billy smiles. Waits a bit.

"Fuck you."

"Well, that ain't rightly conducive to a civilized conversation. Is it?"

Billy doesn't answer. Thinks, I might like this cop.

"All right, Pilgrim. But you're not goin' to last very long up there without a bit of a patch job. You know that. I know that."

More silence.

"You'd rather die than go to the pokey, fine by me."

Billy laughs. 'The pokey.'

"I can wait you out. I got patience. 'Course you might pass out and I'll haul your ass away anyhow."

Billy doesn't respond. No need.

"How about this? Give us your name so we can notify your next of kin, however this turns out."

Billy laughs. Out loud this time. It hurts. He doubles over. Clutches his stomach. Hurts so bad. A moan escapes.

"Pilgrim? You still there?"

"Long as you are."

"Don't bet on it."

Something moves. Billy's peripheral vision. He turns. Aims.

A cat. Scruffy looking. Silver tabby. Black tiger stripes over gray. Where did it come from? How did it get here? No clue.

Cat tiptoes to Billy. Nonchalant. Stealthy. Circles him.

"You want to throw your life away like this, son?"

"Life is cheap. Living costs you. And don't call me 'son'."

Billy lies back again. Gun in hand. Cat squats. Eyes him. Billy watches back.

Hours seep past. Maybe minutes. Helicopter returns. Hauling a column of light underneath. Pond of light skitters across pueblo. Stops on Billy. Pinned by light.

Billy shades his eyes. Raises the M-16. Chopper slips away. Takes light island with it.

Cold sucks Billy's body. Dark wearies his mind. Cat rubs against his leg. Billy thankful for the warmth. Billy's eyes close. He forces them open. His lids fall.

"Mama?"

Billy wakes at the sound. Scared. Who said that? Slaps his wound with his pistol. Breath hisses between clenched teeth. Awake now. Tears of pain cloud his eyes.

Where did pistol come from. Did he carry it up here? Oh, was in jacket pocket.

Hears a radio. A song. Roy Orbison. Loneliest voice ever. Roy echoes around the pueblo.

The east sky lightens. Sun stains the horizon. Orange. Black shadows creep across the pueblo.

Cat snuggled into bent knee.

Billy reaches hand to the cat. To pet. Hand trembles. Stares at own hand. Curious. Not like it's his. Flexes.

Notices the blood. All around him. A large pool. Has he any left? How much time left?

"Who's the baddest motherfucker in this joint?" he whispers. Smiles. Smells stale beer and wine. Wants a Coke with cherry juice. That would be heaven. Laughs. Out loud. Heaven.

"Pilgrim, you still with us?

"Still here."

"No offense, but…you don't sound so good."

"I think I'm catching a cold."

The cat unfurls. Steps into the blood. Laps it from curled paws. Billy flaps his hand. Shoos it away. Cat retreats.

"Was mighty chilly last night. Bet you're hungry. We got hot coffee down here."

"No offense sheriff, but…fuck off, please."

Billy struggles to his knees. Falls. Rises again. Roars with the pain. Stands. The cops below stare. Must be a hundred of them now.

Fires the M-16. Empties a magazine at a cloud. Takes pistol shots at the sun.

The guns below respond. Billy is hit. Arms, leg, chest. Body twitches, jerks. Falls. To his knees.

Sees the ladder return. World tilts. Billy on side now. Cops charge onto the roof. Billy watches. Gun kicked away from his hands.

Billy can't breathe. Foamy scarlet pumps out chest holes. Eyes won't focus.

Sun is blotted out. The sheriff?

"Why'd you do it, Pilgrim? We outnumber you. Nowhere to go. You never had a chance."

Billy wants to laugh. Coughs instead. Spews blood. Pain goes away. He just grins to himself.

Never had a….

# ABOUT THE AUTHOR

Patrick Sheane Duncan is an American writer, film producer and director.

A graduate of Grand Valley State University in Allendale Charter Township, Michigan, Duncan's career has been influenced by his Vietnam War experiences, which inspired the television mini-series *Vietnam War Story* (1987) and its sequel *Vietnam War Story: The Last Days* (1989) and the films *84C MoPic* (1989) and *Courage Under Fire* (1996). Additional writing credits include *A Home of Our Own* (1993), *The Pornographer* (1994), *Nick of Time* (1995), *Mr. Holland's Opus* (1995), and the television movies *A Painted House* (2003), *Elvis* (2005), and *The Little Red Wagon* (2012).

Duncan is a winner of the CableACE Award for Writing for a Dramatic Series for *Vietnam War Story: The Last Days* and a Christopher Award for *Mr. Holland's Opus*, which also garnered him a Golden Globe nomination. He was nominated for the Grand Jury Prize at the Sundance Film Festival for *84C MoPic* and *The Pornographer* and the Independent Spirit Award for Best First Feature and Best Screenplay for *84C MoPic*.

Duncan's play, *Souls on Fire*, was produced by Danny Glover's theatre company, Robey Theatre Company in Los Angeles.